And what if something happens to my stars?

Henry's Big Star Adventure

Dark Canyon Stars Publishing

ISBN-10: 0-99-0983439
ISBN-13: 978-0-9909834-3-9
Text copyright © 2015 by Scott Schumaker.
Illustrations copyright © 2015 by Jason Okutake.

HENRY'S
Big Star Adventure

Written by Scott Schumaker
Illustrated by Jason Okutake

"The nitrogen in our DNA, the calcium in our teeth, the iron in our blood, the carbon in our apple pies were made in the interiors of collapsing stars. We are made of star stuff."

—*Carl Sagan, Cosmos*

Crash!

Chapter 1

Henry froze and looked over his shoulder.

The hallway table he'd just run into was still wobbling, but the large snow globe that had been sitting on top wasn't there. Instead water and bits of fake snow and splinters of glass were oozing down the walls and making puddles on the floor. The nature scene that had been inside—a family of rams climbing a mountain, and geese flying west into a sunset—had shattered too.

"Ah man!" Henry said, pressing his fists into his face. He pulled his fists down his cheeks, giving himself droopy zombie eyes.

His mom's voice echoed through his head: *How many times do I have to tell you not to chase Lion in the house? Don't run in the house! Stop chasing the cat! You're going to break something. Break something. Break something.*

"Idiot," Henry said to himself.

"*Idiot* is rather harsh," said a voice behind him. "But, you, sir, *are* in trouble."

Henry pivoted, causing his red high-tops to squeak on the wood floor, and his mop of hair to flop against his head. There was no one there, only

Lion. The cat looked up at Henry with a blank stare, the tuft of hay-yellow fur around her neck framing her face like a sunflower.

Henry squinted, baffled. Being called *sir* by anyone was strange enough. *Sir* was for old people. He was just a kid. Regardless, he was completely, absolutely, positively sure a cat should not being calling him *sir*. Cats could not talk. Or, at least he had been completely, absolutely, positively sure cats could not talk until five seconds ago.

Lion fanned her tail and, spying her favorite toy at the far end of the hallway—a shabby sock full of catnip—began to stalk it as if it were a mouse.

"No way," Henry muttered. "Cats can't talk."

The cat pounced on the sock, batted it with her one white paw and gave chase, causing the pink bell tied under her neck to jingle and jangle.

Henry looked back at the mess on the floor and walls, and realized two things: one, that he shouldn't be hanging around the crime scene, and, two, that debating the talking ability of his cat was pointless, because cats couldn't talk! With that he bolted to his room.

Chapter 2

"For crying out loud!" Henry heard his mom exclaim. His parents had just come into the house from cleaning the garage. "Henry Cornwall!"

"Ah man!" Henry mumbled, swinging the space ship in his hand through a low arc.

It was dark now and he had yet to think of a good excuse for the broken snow globe. In fact, he had been doing his best not to think about it at all. He'd spent a good twenty minutes bouncing on his bed trying unsuccessfully to perfect a front flip with a twist. Another half hour had been spent drawing a platoon of zorkalorks. Then he'd spent at least five minutes prying open his sticky window when his room had begun to feel as if it were a million degrees. His mom never turned on the air conditioning unless it felt at least a million and twenty degrees inside the house. It was then he'd decided it must have been the growing windstorm outside—the one making the house creak—that had sounded like someone talking, *not* his cat. Now he was playing with a toy space ship.

Henry was pretending to be the space ship's captain, zooming from star to star, planet to planet, battling aliens and saving the universe. He kept playing despite his mom having just used her you're-in-trouble voice

because he thought he might not get in trouble if he acted as if nothing were wrong.

"Henry?" boomed his dad.

"Crud," he whispered. "In here."

Their footsteps sounded like thunder coming down the hall, and Henry's stomach balled up in knots. Getting in trouble again would mean another week of no TV, no video games, and no playing soccer after dinner. Dessert would get cut off too. His life would be ruined.

He wished one of their phones would ring, or the doorbell. Either of those might distract his parents and give him enough time to think of a decent excuse. Or, even better, the house could catch fire. His parents would forget all about the snow globe if the house caught fire.

They appeared in the doorway.

"Henry," his mom said, "did you break the snow globe?" She didn't look mad. She looked sad. The knots in Henry's stomach began feeling heavy, as if soaked in water. In that moment he decided houses never caught fire when you need them to.

Henry and his mom shared the same round nose and sawdust-colored hair, but he'd gotten his Dad's blue eyes and long, slender fingers. His dad was drumming those long fingers across his biceps, arms crossed. Henry didn't have to look to see his father's stern face, the one Henry always felt could vaporize him at any moment.

Instead Henry focused on the dirty round purple sneakers his mom was wearing, the ones she always wore to clean the garage. He thought they made her feet look like enormous smashed grapes.

"No. Wasn't me." Henry shook his head. His hand began taking the space ship through a series of increasingly faster loops and dips.

His dad raised his eyebrows and pursed his lips. "Mmmhmm. Any idea what happened then?"

"Uhh," Henry said. His brain was blank. His stomach felt as if it were doing soggy cartwheels. His tongue felt as if a furry ball were stuck in his throat. He squinched up his eyes, preparing to confess, when he spied Lion's catnip-filled sock and had an idea.

"I, uh, I heard Lion running all over the place," he said. "She was chasing something, probably a mouse. You should, you should set some traps or something around here, Dad. And then I heard this really, really, *reeeally* big crash. I think Lion broke it!"

His parents looked at each other. They didn't say a thing, but his mom gave his dad a slight nod, which his dad returned. Henry hated when they did this. It was as if they had some sort of parental superpower that allowed them to talk to each other without saying a word. This, in Henry's opinion, was completely, absolutely, positively unfair. The space ship in his hand was zooming left, right, up and down as fast as his hand could carry it.

They looked back at him.

"I *suppose*," said his mom as his parents' faces relaxed. "Get ready for bed then. It's getting late."

They turned to leave, closing the door behind them. But as they did, Lion slipped in, gliding past Henry's mom's purple shoes.

Chapter 3

Henry took the space ship through a big slow loop and brought it in for a landing. He sighed with relief as he watched Lion strut across the room and sit in front of him. He couldn't believe his parents had fallen for his story. But, he reminded himself, he was a pretty good storyteller. After all, he'd just written a story about a squirrel, a one-man submarine and a pepperoni pizza, and his teacher had said, "Uh...very inventive, Henry," when she'd handed it back to him with a B+!

The cat stared at him for an uncomfortably long time until Henry said, "What?!"—as if the cat could talk—and a powerful gust of wind blew into the room, ruffling their hair and giving Henry an excuse to break the cat's stare and close the window.

"That was not very nice. You will pay a price," Lion said.

Henry's jaw dropped. He froze and stared at his cat.

Lion continued her rhyme: "You made all that up, saying I was to blame. You lied about me in your fictitious game."

Henry's eyes narrowed. He bit his lower lip. He was about to freak out. He was about to scream. He was about to jump out the window he'd forgotten all about closing.

Instead, a huge *BUUURP!* exploded from his throat. It was so loud it would have silenced his classmates with awe if it'd happened in the school cafeteria. On any other occasion he would have been disappointed that no one else was around to appreciate it's sheer volume, but whatever was now spiraling up his throat behind that hiccup had his undivided attention.

It was warm and ticklish, and when it shot out of his mouth, it floated in front of him, glowing and pulsating white. It danced a little jig between Henry and Lion as if deciding what to do, and then zipped out the window while Henry watched transfixed, unable to say anything more than "I...eer...eek...auk."

He crinkled his nose and shook his head in disbelief until the white globe disappeared into the night sky. He jerked his head back towards Lion and said, "Wait a second! You *can* talk?!"

"Of course I can talk," Lion said, matter of fact. Her voice was dignified and confident. "I am, after all, a very wise cat. 'Til now I've just had nothing to say, such as: I will be blamed for your lie by your mom and dad, and you... well, you will be a little more sad."

Henry's head swiveled back and forth between Lion and the stars outside. "You're crazy. I'm happy as ice cream," he stammered.

"You mean you are *as* happy *as* when you are *eating* ice cream," Lion replied. "And yes, indeed that is the way it may seem. But I know you just saw that white thing float away, and—*meow*—that was part of your heart 'til today."

"What? That can't happen. Can it? It can't, right?" Henry put a hand on his chest; his heart was still there, still beating. But anything seemed possible at that moment. His cat was talking to him for crying out loud! "This is all *so* totally weird," he said, sitting down on the floor with a thud.

Lion said, "Oh, yes, as you know, your heart is a muscle and makes your blood flow. But, there's something else in there few know or recall:

Extra-small stars fill your heart when you're born, like snowflakes in a ball."

"You mean star-stars?" Henry said, raising his eyebrows and pointing to the sky. "Like those?"

"Indeed," said Lion, sighing as if all this were as obvious as the nose on Henry's face. "Sometimes when you're hurt, but more so when you're mean, stars will jump off your heart like pinballs in a machine."

"Remember that time you called your friend Tess an ugly crawdad and pushed her down on the ground because you were mad? You lost quite a few stars at the end of that race. All because those boys teased you for not winning first place? Yet now she has stitches, her knee is all black and blue. Your folks did the right thing when they grounded you."

"How'd you know all that about Tess? And the other kids at school?" Henry asked. Sometimes he wished his family would move to a new town. That's how mean some of the other boys in his class were.

***

Henry hadn't meant to make Tess fall. They lived on the same street and had been friends forever.

Tess was a half year older than Henry and never missed an opportunity to point it out. She was tall and gawky, and always carried a baton—always.

The other kids called her "ostrich" or "Amazon" or "freak," just as they teased Henry with "klutzoid" or "Cornball."

Despite her gawkiness, Tess could run. And that day in the schoolyard, her long auburn hair was flowing every which direction behind her as they raced along the chainlink fence that separated the school from a lake. They were halfway down the fence when Tess began pulling ahead, her hair dancing all over the place, almost as if taunting Henry.

Henry lost big time. To add insult to injury, he snagged his foot on a

root right after the finish and crashed face first into the dirt. All the boys watching at the finish line keeled over in heckling hysterics—"Cornball got beat by a girl! Klutzoid got beat by a girl!" Tess, meanwhile, had her hands on her knees and was catching her breath. She smiled, shrugged and whispered, "Sorry, snail legs."

Then one of the boys kicked dirt in his face.

Henry exploded, but not at the boy who'd kicked the dirt. He was bigger and stronger than Henry.

"Shut up, you ugly crawdad!" Henry yelled and he launched himself off the ground with all his might and barreled into Tess.

When she fell, her knee hit a rock and exploded with blood.

She ended up getting seven stitches. Henry ended up grounded.

***

Lion delicately licked her lips before answering Henry's question: "As I said, I'm a very wise cat, and your parents talked a lot about that. Now, allow me to finish explaining all this. It really is something you just should not miss."

Henry sat back on his heels and knocked on his head with his fist as if it would help him understand how his cat was talking. He gave Lion his full attention.

"Each and every time you were mean, your heart lost a star as you have just seen. And the same does happen when someone hurts you. That is, you lose a star, sometimes even two. And each time a star floats up and away, you get a little less happy, a little more gray. You won't get really sad right away, it is true, but someday you'll wake up feeling unhappy—what grown-ups call blue."

"Why do you rhyme everything?" Henry said.

"Oh," said Lion. Raising her eyebrows and cocking her head to the right, she cleared her throat. "Yes, I suppose I was. Old habit, really. I learned to talk by listening to your mother read you nursery rhymes when you were small. I simply detested the ones where the princess *always* had to be saved by the prince. Pah! I see absolutely no reason the prince could not have needed saving every now and then. Anyway, my apologies for what I imagine were some dreadful rhymes. I will cease and desist immediately."

Henry said, "I...I...I'll just keep my mouth shut when any of that stuff happens, and hold my stars in."

"No, sorry," Lion replied. "Nice try and that's good creative thinking, just like that story with the pepperoni pizza and the submarine and the squirrel."

"You can read too?"

Lion smiled and shrugged as if it were no big deal, then continued. "But those stars. They are tricky. Sometimes they come straight out like that one did, but usually they wait until you're asleep or not paying attention. And if they can't get out one way they find another."

"Uh, what do you mean?" Henry wasn't sure whether he really wanted to know the answer.

"If they can't come out through a burp or a hiccup, they might come out your nose or your ears, or, if need be, they'll come shooting right out your rear."

Henry winced and put one hand over his mouth and nose and the other on the seat of his shorts.

"I want my stars back," Henry declared, his words muffled.

Lion replied, "Are you sure about tha—*Ack! Ack! Ack!*"

She coughed, put a paw over her mouth and turned her head towards the wall. "So sorry, hairball."

Henry didn't notice. He dropped his hand from his face. "Yes! I'm completely, absolutely, positively sure I want my stars back!"

"Now see here: There's no need to yell and quack," Lion said. "No one likes a screamiac."

"But I don't want to be sad or blue or whatever," Henry said. His forehead was wrinkled with concern. "And what if something happens to my stars? Like an alien attacks them and blows them up with a death ray? Or they get sucked down a black hole or crushed by an asteroid or something?"

"Henry, again," Lion said, "there is no need to yell. Your stars will be safe."

"Why?"

"Because, you see, the sky will guard your stars until you ascend."

"What's *ascend*?" Henry asked. His brain felt twisted and strained. This was all even more bizarre than where babies came from.

"*Ascend* means to 'climb or rise,' which is what you must do to get your stars back. And once you hold those stars again, what happens next is really quite grand. Assuming you survive the trip, that is."

"Really?" Henry said, not even hearing Lion's last sentence. "I get to go into space? Awesome! I am so ready." Visions of astronauts and flying a space ship across the galaxy tumbled through Henry's head.

Lion said, "You will have to be brave—and really, keep your voice down. If your parents find out I can talk, my lovely, tranquil life will be ruined. There will be TV and radio interviews to do, book deals, movie deals, commercials, and—"

"I am brave," whispered Henry, cutting Lion off and sitting up straight. "Like an astronaut...or a pirate."

"Hmm," Lion said, her tail swishing idly side to side. "We'll see. The true test of your courage will be when you're alone. But if, as you say, you're ready to go, what you first must do is crawl under your bed."

Henry's mouth fell open and his face turned a purplish blue.

"Are you bonkers? Crawl under my bed? No way!"

Chapter 4

"No way am I going under my bed," Henry said, exasperated. "Uh-uh. Not happening."

"And why would that be?" Lion said.

"Zorkalorks."

"Zorkadorks?" Lion peered under the bed. "What on Earth is a zorkadork?"

"Zork*alorks*," Henry said. He reached across the floor and grabbed his drawing of the zorkalorks. "They're huge and they're hairy and they stink like dirty cheese, and they're strong as ten gorillas, and they've got big pointy heads and big claws and razor-sharp teeth."

"And you're scared of them? I thought you were as brave as an astronaut."

"Yeah, I'm scared of them, and an astronaut would be too. They'd tear an astronaut apart in about five seconds. You'd be crazy *not* to be scared of them, 'specially at night. That's when I see their shadows on my walls. And hear them singing. Mom says I'm imagining it. But I'm not. I know I'm not."

"Singing?" Lion said.

"Yeah. They sound like a bunch of toads getting stepped on," Henry said. He stood with his hands over his head like claws, and gave himself a deep toady voice:

Ook-ah-ew!
Time for cookies and tea!
When we find you,
we eat you, Henry!

"Cookie and tea? Strange," Lion said, walking towards the bed. "They must be British."

"Huh?" Henry said in his normal voice.

"Never mind. So why haven't they?"

"Why haven't they what?"

"Eaten you."

"Because they don't see me. Duh." Henry splayed out both his hands towards Lion to emphasize how completely obvious that was. "I get under my covers and don't move or make any noise."

"I see," Lion said, walking towards the bed. "Wait here. I'll take a look."

"What?!" Henry cried. "No!" He reached for Lion, but the cat had already disappeared into the darkness under the bedframe.

Outside Henry's window another gust of wind blew, this one even stronger than the last. The trees in the backyard groaned and rattled under its force, and when it blustered in through the window, it lifted the sheets off of the bed. It even wrapped itself around Henry, knocking him off balance. Henry steadied himself by putting a hand on the rug but didn't move to close the window. He was focused on the charcoal-dark gap between the bed and the floor.

A coyote howled on a far hillside, and the lights in his room flickered and buzzed.

Henry kept waiting and staring.

The longer he stared, the more certain he became that Lion was already the meat filling in a freshly made zorkalork sandwich. And suddenly he worried that by sitting on the floor he was an easy target.

Something rustled under the bed. Henry looked up at his covers. There was no way he'd make it under them in time from where he sat.

"Lion?" he whispered, scooting away from the bed. Goosebumps twisted up his spine.

"Just lint under there and an old piece of clay," Lion said casually, strolling out from the end of the bed.

Henry gasped.

"Surprised? Ha. No zorkalork is going to eat me. I am quiet as a whisper and fast as the dickens." Lion smiled and spoke with such confidence, Henry felt silly he had worried at all. He wished he could be more like his cat.

"What's a dickens?"

"I have no idea," Lion said. "Regardless, I saw no zorkalorks or three-legged gobblygoks or headless bogeymen or anything of that sort under there. The coast, as they say, appears to be clear."

Henry swallowed hard. He knew that meant it was his turn to go.

Chapter 5

Henry ducked low and looked under the bed. Squinting into the darkness, he said, "Are you sure there's nothing under there?"

"Most certain," Lion said. "Still scared, are you?"

"Maybe. A little, yeah."

Lion said, "I am sure you are. In fact, I would find it odd if you were not. However, remember, even those pirates you admire would get anxious when one yelled, 'Land ho!' Part of that was the thrill of dropping anchor on an unexplored land, but another part of it was that they had no idea what dangers they'd face. They had no idea what kind of villainous thieves or ravenous beasts or man-eating moss they might come across."

"Man-eating moss?" said Henry.

"Oh yes. Vile stuff. Fluorescent green and brown. Orange openings all over it, each one filled with hundreds of little teeth. Regardless, despite being scared—which of course they'd never admit to each other, because heaven forbid that two men open up to each other and share their true feelings—they had to stay brave to find their treasure. As do you to find yours. Your stars, that is."

Lion took a moment to grab hold of the carpet with her front paws and stretch before strutting around the room, inspecting its contents.

"Of course," she continued, "they also had cannons and were excellent swordsmen. Or at least the ones who lived a long time tended to be excellent swordsmen. But you cannot very well carry a cannon, now can you? There is no way you'd be able to hold it. You'd end up dropping it on your toes, squishing them like raspberries."

Henry grew excited. "Do I get a sword? A sword would be *most* premium." He grabbed a pencil from the floor and sallied around the room pretending it was a cutlass and he was battling a massive zorkalork.

"'Most premium'?" Lion said, raising an eyebrow. "Where in the world did you pick that up?"

"Tess's brother. He plays guitar in a band and drives a Mustang," Henry said as he continued his imaginary duel.

"The lexicon of youth...fascinating," Lion said, apparently talking to herself, since, despite Henry's baffled look, she did not offer to explain that *lexicon* means "vocabulary." "Well, regardless," the cat continued, "a sword is out of the question, and for the nine lives of me, I will never understand you males and your fascination with weapons."

Henry, about to impale the imaginary zorkalork, stopped his duel in mid-thrust and dropped his hands in disappointment. "Aw, c'mon, *please*."

"No. You're too young, not to mention clumsy. The very thought of you with a razor-sharp instrument of death gives me indigestion."

"I'm not clumsy," Henry protested.

"Now, there's no need to get your underwear all tied up in a knot," Lion replied. "Boys your age tend to be clumsy, that's all. Some, like you, are more clumsier than others. It's just the way it works until you stop growing and your body can get used to itself."

"Oh," Henry said, looking at the floor. Then he had a thought. "Hold on. Why do I even need anything? You just said there wasn't anything under

there but lint."

"And an old piece of clay," said Lion as she jumped onto the bed. Without answering his question she continued, "Therefore, hold on to that pencil and grab that jump rope off the floor." Lion pointed to each item with a single claw as she named it. "The flashlight in your drawer and...tsk, tsk, and you wonder why your mother is always telling you to clean your drawers."

Henry looked in the drawer as he grabbed his flashlight. "It's not *that* messy."

Lion purred and replied, "And *I'm* not a cat who talks in rhyme. Now, what else?"

The cat's gaze next fell on the gigantic leaf tacked on Henry's wall. It was a banana leaf as long as Henry was tall. His parents had brought it back from a vacation in Costa Rica and he'd once taken it to show-and-tell. His classmates hadn't thought it was as cool as he did. Actually, at recess, they'd said the leaf was lame and called him a loser.

Henry looked at Lion. "The leaf? Are you a nutball?"

Lion laughed. It was dainty and breathy, like the sound a hundred daisies would make if they opened and closed quickly at the same time.

"Trust me," Lion said. "Take it."

Lion smiled a sly cat smile that gave Henry the impression she knew more than she was saying. More goosebumps flashed down his arms and across the back of his neck as Lion resumed talking. "And last but not least, take my bell."

She held up her head up to better expose the bell on her collar.

"But it's *pink*," said Henry, pronouncing *pink* as if it were *puke*.

"Yes, I know it's pink. Your mother seems to think that simply because I'm a female cat she should reinforce male/female stereotypes and bejewel me with something pink. I would have preferred cobalt blue or perhaps fire-engine red. But that does not matter. You must take it."

Henry crossed his arms and remained where he was.

Lion said, "No one will be able to see what color it is if you put it in one of your pockets." The cat nodded towards the dirt-smudged olive green shorts Henry was wearing. They drooped below his knees and were hung with multiple pockets.

Henry reluctantly uncrossed his arms. "Fine, whatever," he huffed. He didn't want a stupid little pink bell to keep him from becoming an astronaut.

As he untied the bell, Lion said, "Now, if you truly and absolutely get stuck, ring it and holler."

Henry gave Lion a quizzical look. "Holler what?"

"Why whatever comes out your mouth when you start ringing it, of course."

"I have *absolutely* no idea what you're talking about," Henry said, shaking his head. He pulled the chair from the desk to the wall. Climbing atop it, he untacked the leaf, then jumped down and tied one end of the jump rope to the tip of the leaf, and the other end to the leaf's stem. Lion nodded with apparent approval as Henry slung the rope over his shoulder.

Henry put a hand in each of his pockets to confirm everything else was securely inside. "Pencil? Check. Flashlight? Check? Girly, pukey pink bell? Check."

Lion rolled her eyes and said, "Are you ready to go?"

Henry looked at stars outside his bedroom window. He drew in a deep breath, held it, and exhaled. "I guess so," he said as he lay down on his belly near the edge of the bed.

"Hello?" he whispered. "Any zorkalorks under here?"

"I told you there were none," Lion said flatly.

Henry still waited for an answer.

He heard no reply. He took a deep breath, and he plunged his head into the darkness. Once his eyes adjusted to the dimness, he could make out balls of lint and the dry piece of clay. The clay had rolled under the bed last May. He'd been too afraid a zorkalork would snatch him to get it back.

He swallowed hard and checked again for the pencil. He figured that at least it was sharp. He might be able to use it to poke out a zorkalork's eye, or jam it down an ear or up a nose.

"OK. Here goes," he said, and wiggled the rest of his body underneath the bed.

Chapter 6

Henry lay there in the dark, trying not to make any noise, but dust began to tickle his nose. He scrunched his left cheek and eye together, then his right cheek and eye, then his whole face as he tried to scrunch the sneeze out of existence.

"Ah-chooo!"

Henry froze and waited to be eaten.

"Gesundheit," Lion said calmly from on top of the bed. The cat's words were followed by a licking noise that Henry recognized as Lion cleaning herself. He found this reassuring. Lion was bathing. She was completely unconcerned that anything might happen. The licking stopped long enough for Lion to say, "How are you doing down there?"

"OK, I think." Henry's relief at not immediately becoming a zorkalork snack was turning into a spark of confidence. "Nothing under here but lint and that piece of—What the heck?" Henry watched as a fast-moving dribble of water raced across the floor and under his palm. He wiped his hand on his shorts.

Groping along the floor, he found the leak's source—a crack near the wall. He was about to yell, "Daaaad! My bedroom's leaking!" when the trickle of water exploded into a raging torrent.

At the same moment an incredible gust of wind stormed through the window and blew straight under the bed. It was so strong that Henry could barely catch his breath, much less call for help. It was so strong that it seemed to grab Henry like a giant hand, spinning him around and pushing him towards the water.

Henry scratched at the floor, grasping for something to hold onto. His fingernails caught on the edge of a floorboard, halting his slide just as his feet plunked into the rushing water. He strained to maintain his fingerhold, gritting his teeth and trying to get his feet out of the water.

The wind kicked up another notch.

"Whoooaaaa!"

Henry plunged into the water and found that what a moment ago had been the floor was now deep, deep water.

He tried screaming for help, but his voice was garbled by the rushing current. He caught a glimpse of Lion's shadow on the wall just beyond the bed. She must have heard all the noise, he thought. One of her ears even looked to be twitching back and forth, listening, but she continued cleaning herself as if nothing were happening.

A moment later the wall and Lion's shadow disappeared as water rushed over his head. Henry grabbed for the surface, only to have the jagged edge of floorboards scratch his arms. He felt himself falling; everything was a swirl of darkness and water. His chest began to squeeze in on itself. He was running out of air.

***

Splosh!

His freefall ended. He bobbed to the surface, gasping for air as a raging

river grabbed him and sent him shooting downstream fast as a rocket. Henry was too confused and scared to remember that the pink bell in his pocket might somehow help him.

As it was, he could just barely make out the edge of the very large cave downriver. Its mouth looked like a moonless, starless night, only ten times darker.

"Holy cannoli! *Argh!*" he screamed as he struggled to swim across the current, straining to keep his head above the water, hoping to catch a glimpse of a riverbank. It was useless. The current clutched him like a piece of driftwood.

Then he heard a voice.

"Henry, be brave."

It sounded like Lion's voice, but he couldn't be sure with all the water hissing and boiling in his ears, tumbling him in every direction. He was turned upside down and right side up before he heard the voice again. It said, "To get your stars back, watch out for the signs. They will guide you on this journey."

Water rushed down his throat and he began coughing and hacking.

The voice continued: "And if zorkalorks attack, here is how to have a fair fight. Take a huge breath. Draw it down deep inside you. Take aim at a zorkalork and blow. Blow with all your might while making this sound like a siren: ZEEEEWWWW."

Henry *had* to ask the voice a question now, but a wave dunked him. He fought his way back to the surface.

"What the heck will"—*hack, hack, cough!*—"that do?" he cried, spitting water, his voice desperate and afraid.

The voice didn't answer. It was too late. Henry had dropped into the cave.

Chapter 7

The river began dropping faster and steeper, and when Henry could get enough air to scream—"AIIIIGGGHHH!"—his screams echoed through the cave: "AIIIIGGGHHH! AIIIIGGGHHH! AIIIIGGGHHH! AIIIIGGGHHH!"

But the voice had said to be brave. So Henry forced himself to stop screaming in mid-howl: "AIII..."

Henry waited to feel braver.

He didn't. He was still certain that if the water didn't kill him, something in the darkness would.

Once, a few years ago, he and his mom had gone into a huge department store and gotten separated, and he'd gotten lost. He'd thought that was about as scared as he could ever possibly be. He'd been wrong. Way wrong.

Something jabbed him sharp in the back.

"Aiiiiggghhh!" he screamed, jolting halfway out of the river.

He was certain it was a zorkalork. He was certain this was it and he was about to be torn to shreds.

It stabbed him again, harder, causing his whole body to jerk as he jammed his eyes shut and clenched his jaw. He waited for the zorkalork's razor-sharp teeth to rip through him.

Then it flip-flopped against his back.

Henry opened one eye cautiously. That didn't seem right, he thought: zorkalorks couldn't flip-flop. He was certain. They were too big and fat and hairy.

He took hold of the jump rope and whirled around. "But a banana leaf could!" he yelled, and behind him the leaf was bobbing and flopping on the water.

"Duh, stupid," he said, squinting at the leaf and realizing a zorkalork wouldn't even bother jabbing him in the first place—it would just rip him apart without warning.

Something about the leaf was different, though. Henry squinted harder, trying to make out the leaf's entire shape in the darkness. It was three times its original size.

"*No way,*" Henry said, shocked by not only by its size but by how much it resembled a boat.

Untying one end of the rope and wrapping it around his wrist, he grabbed hold of the leaf's stem. It was so fat that he couldn't get his hands all the way around it as he pulled himself up onto the leaf.

The leaf wibbled and wobbled and almost tipped over, but it kept floating even with all of Henry's weight on it.

Awesome, Henry thought, as he steadied himself and stood up.

The leaf dove to one side, and Henry dropped back down onto his belly.

"Jeesh!" he exclaimed. He rewrapped the rope around his wrist, tighter this time. He didn't want to lose the leaf if he fell back into the water.

He moved towards the center of the leaf once more, this time on his hands and knees, imagining he was a ninja slipping deftly into his enemy's hideout. He hoped the leaf wouldn't tear apart under his weight. Each time he moved forward the leaf collapsed inward, swallowing his legs and arms. It was like crawling across a giant jellyfish.

"Cool," Henry said with a sigh of relief after he'd wibbled and wobbled to the center and plopped down cross-legged. But he still couldn't see anything. He could only feel the leaf spinning its way down the river, the darkness wrapped around him as tight as a blindfold. He wasn't a big fan of absolute darkness, especially while floating down a crazy underground river on a gigantic leaf with who knows what creeping, slithering, and swimming around below him.

"Flllllashlight!" Henry said, jabbing his finger in the air with verve.

He crammed his hand into his pocket and felt the flashlight's cold metal casing.

"Yeesss."

He pulled it out, and gobs of water drained from the casing.

"Noooo."

He flicked its switch back and forth. Nothing.

"C'mon. C'mon. C'mon."

He flicked it back and forth, back and forth. Nothing. Nothing. He felt hot tears rising behind his eyelids. It was as useless as a bicycle without pedals.

He started to cry. He didn't care about being brave anymore. He didn't care about his stars. He didn't care whether everyone from school suddenly fell out of the black void and saw him crying and made fun of him and called him a loser crybaby. He just wanted the darkness to end, and to get off the river. And to be home. And to be in his room. And to have his mom and dad tucking him into bed.

The leaf pirouetted and rolled through another set of rapids, bouncing off unseen rocks and pitching Henry across the leaf. Tears rolled down his face like marbles as he made desperate grabs for any part of the leaf that offered a hold. He was certain the darkness was going to last forever.

Until it didn't.

He was still crying and holding onto the leaf for dear life when something caught his eye—a faint, blurry red glow downriver. He wiped at his tears and looked again.

The glow was still there, brighter now.

He shut his eyes tight and opened them. The light was still there, getting brighter.

And brighter.

Henry threw his hands in the air and screamed, "Hallelujah!"

He jumped unto the leaf and spun out a dance, spinning so fast that his shorts almost fell off.

"Whoa," he said, grabbing his shorts and collapsing in a happy heap onto the leaf. He caught his breath and watched the red light continue to grow stronger. He noticed that the river was slowing. If it kept slowing down, he thought, he might be able to paddle out of the current.

He was so jubilant, so relieved, that he couldn't help but dance again. This time, though, he kept his feet firmly planted as the leaf wrapped itself up to his knees. He moved only his hips and arms and bobbed his head—"Yay! Yay! Yay! I'm gonna live!"—his shaggy hair jumping in every direction. He looked like a cornstalk being blown every which way in the wind.

***

That was, until he heard the singing. Someone or something—in fact, many someones or somethings—were singing, repeating the same verses over and over.

He got on his hands and knees and strained forward, trying to make out the words.

No, he thought, not now. No. It couldn't be.

His heart skipped a beat. His face went pale and cold.

The voices sounded like someone stepping on a chorus of toads.

They were singing:

Ook-ah-ew!
Cookies and tea!
Me eat you
if you don't eat me!

Chapter 8

The singing was coming from downriver, the same as the light, from around a curve in the cave that bent to the right. Knots began forming everywhere in Henry's stomach. He started paddling ferociously and uselessly in the other direction. Now he wanted nothing more than to get back into the darkness and hide.

His heart began pounding so hard he thought it was going to pop right through his chest. He lay down on the leaf and tried to conceal himself within its soft folds. He wished he had never listened to Lion. He wished he'd never gone under his bed. He wished he'd never pushed Tess or lied about breaking the snow globe.

He and the leaf swung around the bend and entered an enormous cavern. His eyes bugged out. His whole body tensed as if it'd been struck by lightning. The cavern was as big as three football fields and infested with zorkalorks, hundreds of them.

"Lion!" he gasped through gritted teeth. *"You call this no zorkalorks?!"*

He wanted to jump up and curse his cat, curse her so badly that his parents would have grounded him through high school. Instead he stayed as stiff as concrete.

The zorkalorks were larger than he had imagined. They were running in crazy circles on both sides of the river, chasing each other and jumping through the brilliant red bonfires that blazed and crackled throughout the cavern. They grabbed and clawed at each other, clacking their teeth and licking their lips, and singing:

Ook-ah-ew!
Cookies and tea!
Me eat you
if you don't eat me!

Henry spied a lone zorkalork on a high ledge. This zorkalork was even bigger than the rest, and stood with the claws of his toes curled over the edge. He was holding a huge burning stump in one of his enormous paws. A sinister, amused grin was plastered across his face as he watched the other zorkalorks chase each other. A gong as wide as Henry's bedroom hung behind the monster.

The beast dug into his ear, pulled out a spiny-backed bug that had at least one thousand legs, and popped the insect into his mouth like a piece of cheese. Crunching it up, the monster let out a deep thunderous burp and, looking very pleased with himself, held up the burning stump with both paws and struck the gong.

Bonggg!

All the zorkalorks stopped chasing each other and dropped to the ground. Henry watched, confused, as they began doing pushups and chanting:

With each pushup me get strong
Me do ten at every gong.
See me arms so big and mighty
so me can squash things small and flighty.

Henry caught his breath. He was certain that he qualified as something small and flighty.

The monsters popped back onto their feet, roared, gave each other high fives and belly slams, then resumed chasing each other and singing in their toady voices—except the zorkalorks who had previously been doing the chasing were now the ones being chased. The closest any of them ever got to catching each other was snatching a pawful of hair off the back of whichever monster they were chasing. This gave the slower zorkalorks a spattering of furless polka dots from their necks to their tails.

Henry strained his face, horrified. He realized they weren't trying to eat each other at all—they were practicing how to catch things, so when the time came to catch something small and flighty, they'd be ready. He flattened himself even deeper into the leaf and wished the river would turn fast and dark again. As it was, it'd slowed to the pace of a lazy slug.

Henry was a quarter of the way through the cavern, thinking he just might pass unnoticed, when the extra-large monster up on the ledge hit the gong again and went to throw himself into a pushup. However, he stopped before hitting the ground.

Bringing both paws to his eyes so he appeared to be staring through hairy binoculars, he leaned far the ledge, peering towards the water. He then jumped backwards with what appeared to be shock, then awe, then excitement. He struck the gong hard and fast—*Bong! Bong! Bong!*—causing the other zorkalorks to pop back to their feet. In a sandpapery voice, the zorkalork proclaimed, "Hooo-ga-who! On big leaf!" He pointed a long claw in Henry's direction. The claw was steely-smooth and glowed red with the reflection of the bonfires.

"*Henry!*" he bellowed.

Chapter 9

The name Henry vibrated through the cavern while the other zorkalorks stood in silence, zeroing in on the leaf. The bonfires sizzled and popped around them.

The monsters' tails began to wiggle and waggle, first one, then another, then the whole gaggle. A few zorkalorks near the river began chanting, "Henry! Henry! Henry!" and stomping their feet. More monsters joined in, then more. Soon they were all chanting his name and smacking their lips and clacking their teeth and stomping up thick clouds of dust.

The zorkalorks nearest the river grabbed snorkels and fins and facemasks from pits dug along the water's edge. Counting off, "One! Two! Three! Four!," they began belly-flopping into the water one by one.

Henry scuttled onto his knees and pulled out his pencil. He held it up in front of him like a knife, his hands shaking. He spun around, trying to figure out which beast was closest. He heard laughter.

The zorkalork on the ledge was roaring with laughter, and when Henry looked up at him, he snarled, "Henry write postcard while us eat Henry? You write, 'Dear Mum, zorkalorks eating me. No be home for dinner.' That what pencil for?"

Henry looked at his pencil and realized it was as likely to fend off a zorkalork as a ham sandwich would be. He cursed Lion again, wishing he had a real sword.

Slipping the pencil back into his pocket, he put his hands back on the leaf to steady himself. The waves from the monsters' belly flops were rolling under the leaf like mini roller coasters.

Take a huge breath, the voice had said. *Take aim at a zorkalork and blow.*

This seemed ridiculous. Blowing at the immense beasts closing in around him was even more absurd than fighting them with a pencil. Still, Henry stood back up on the leaf. He took a deep breath, filling his chest with air. Gasping, he tried to suck in even more. He drew his head back, took aim at the zorkalork closest to him, and let loose. His head snapped forward. His eyes squeezed shut. He felt it in his toes.

He opened one eye, then the other.

The zorkalork was still there, closer now, with an ugly, tooth-filled grin on his face.

"Ah man!" Henry exclaimed. The monster gnashed his teeth, and a spark flew out of his mouth, reminding Henry of the star he'd lost in his room. Getting his stars back now seemed impossible. Ending up inside a zorkalork did not.

And as if the monsters could read Henry's thoughts, their song changed:

Ook-ah-ew!
Cookies and tea!
Me won't eat you,
'cause me eating Henry!

The monster nearest him was now close enough for Henry to see wiry hair covered with slimy goop sprouting out of his ears and nose. He caught a whiff of the zorkalork's scent, and blocked his nose with his fist. It didn't smell like dirty cheese. It smelled like his mom's tuna casserole.

OK, wait, he thought, the voice had said, *Take a huge, deep breath.*

"I did that," Henry said out loud.

The monsters were closing in faster on all sides.

Take it down deep inside of you.

"Did that," Henry said.

Their chanting was getting louder and louder. Henry's whole body was shaking with fear.

Blow at a zorkalork.

"I *did* that!" Henry yelled.

The zorkalork on the ledge was jumping around and doing cartwheels, going berserk.

And make the sound ZEEEEWWWW.

"Right!" Henry said, smacking himself in the forehead with his palm.

Henry took another deep breath down to his toes. He again took aim at the closest monster.

He blew.

Nothing happened.

The zorkalork reached forward to grab the leaf with his big, meaty paw.

Henry added *ZEEEEWWWW.*

The monster shot out of the water and flew across the cavern, slamming into the far wall and falling to the ground in a slump. Henry raised his arms in the air and pumped his fists as if he'd scored a touchdown: "*Yay!*"

Losing no time at all, Henry took aim at the next zorkalork, and the next one, and the next one.

"Aaaaahhhhh...ZEEEEWWWW!
Aaaaahhhhh...ZEEEEWWWW!

43

Aaaaahhhhh...ZEEEEWWWW!"

The air filled with flying zorkalorks and the *thuds* of their bodies slamming into the cavern wall, falling to the ground, knocked out cold. The other zorkalorks began stampeding, trying to escape, tripping and pushing and falling all over each other. They were trying to jam themselves through a few small cracks in the rocks.

Henry was so thoroughly enjoying it all that he didn't see one of them swimming ever-so-quietly up behind him. It was the extra-large zorkalork from the ledge.

He grabbed Henry's leaf and jerked it.

Henry lurched backwards towards the monster, falling onto the leaf right in front of the zorkalork's gaping mouth.

"M'name's Spike," he growled, as the current spun them around. "Henry going to be yum-yum with me cookies and tea."

Henry began to hyperventilate. He couldn't make any sound, much less get a deep breath. Backpedaling away from Spike, the leaf sucking down his every movement, he felt a heavy thunk against his thigh. He reached into his pocket and pulled out the useless flashlight.

Something snapped inside of Henry. There was no thought. There was no fear. Instead, to his surprise, he flung himself back towards Spike. He smashed the beast on the head as hard as he could with the flashlight.

"Hey!" cried the monster, shocked. Spike thrust himself off the leaf, launching it like a torpedo downriver towards the exit of the cavern.

"Ha!" Henry said, holding onto the leaf with all his strength as it shot across the water.

"Owie! That not nice!" Spike blubbered like a baby, gingerly touching the huge welt growing on his head.

"Oh, but eating me is?" Henry yelled back, feeling a surge of confidence. He stuffed the flashlight back into his pocket and as the leaf began to slow, he began paddling as hard and fast as he could. Looking back, he pointed at Spike and cracked, "But hey, thanks for that gigantic push! That was completely, absolutely, positively the best!"

Spike roared and tried to give chase but swallowed a lungful of water instead. The monster began coughing and hacking and spazzing out as Henry paddled the leaf out of the cavern.

The river swung through a series of bends before Henry saw the cave's exit and the sunlight glinting off the water beyond it.

"Yes!" he said, paddling harder.

Once he'd sailed out of the cave, certain he'd left the zorkalorks behind, he collapsed onto the leaf and let the sun's soothing warmth wash across him.

"No one at school is ever going to believe this," he said with an exhausted smile as he faded off to sleep.

He didn't see Spike's snout and stony eyes parting the water like a shark fin far, far behind him.

Chapter 10

Henry woke up to the leaf wheeling slowly in an eddy, bumping into the riverbank. Stretching, he yawned and remembered the voice saying something about following signs to get his stars back. Around him he saw a high grassy bank and a large meadow dazzled with flowers. On the horizon sat the shadow of a gigantic mountain. Behind him the exit to the cavern was nowhere to be seen. He saw no signs of any kind.

"Ah man," Henry moaned, realizing that he not only might have missed a sign but had no idea what they might look like. Or where they might be. For all he knew, they could be hidden under rocks or hanging in trees. What if he never found any of them?

He wished he hadn't fallen asleep. "Stupid. Stupid. Stupid," he said, jumping onto the riverbank and pulling the leaf behind him. Only after he climbed the high bank did he see something poking out of the tall grass. It was a worm-eaten piece of wood shaped like a wedge, nailed to a wobbly stick. Henry could have sworn it had not been there a moment earlier. It pointed down a trail that looked to head to the distant mountain. Written on the sign in big ornate letters was *"THIS WAY, HENRY!"*

Henry's face stretched into a large grin.

"That is a most premium sign," he said. "Even Tess wouldn't miss a sign like that, and she's as dumb as an old piece of twine."

Tess, of course, wasn't dumb. She almost always got straight A's with the exception of English, where the correct use of commas completely baffled her. Henry, meanwhile, got mostly B's no matter how hard he studied, but he *was* a master of the comma.

Henry teased her about being dumb, particularly about commas, just to get her goat, and especially if other boys were around. He didn't want them to think he liked hanging around with Tess. She was a girl, after all, and probably had cooties—not that Henry knew exactly what a cootie was, except that they were gross and he didn't want to catch any and, according to all the guys in his class, girls had them.

It was not ten seconds after Henry declared Tess as dumb as twine that he felt something quiver deep in his ear. It buzzed around in his head before finding its way into his nose. He wondered whether a bee had crept into his ear while he slept and gotten stuck in his head. At this point anything was possible.

He began slamming his hand against the back of his head trying to get it out. But it kept dancing around in his nose until a powerful sneeze climbed up his throat and—*Ah-chooo!*—a star punched its way out of his right nostril.

"Ow!" Henry yelled, rubbing his nose with his palm.

The star circled Henry making a hard chirping noise. It zoomed between his eyes and chirped again, giving Henry the distinct impression he was being reprimanded. Then it floated off in the breeze.

"Jeesh!" Henry said as he watched it rise into the sky.

He made himself a promise right then and there. He held up his right hand as if taking an oath. "If I get my stars back," he said, "I promise to stop calling Tess names." Little electric prickles zinged up his arms and across his back as he spoke, and he felt himself stand a little straighter too.

"That'd be nice," proclaimed a voice behind him.

Henry whirled around and put his hands up in front of himself as he'd seen in kung fu movies. He saw no one. "Who's there?!" he demanded, trying to keep his voice from trembling.

Ten feet off the trail, the tall grass and wildflowers began to quiver. Henry took a step back as something stick-thin and metallic rose out of the field. Attached to its base was a human hand, and attached to that was an arm, and attached to that were a shoulder and a head of auburn hair.

"Tess!" Henry said, dropping his arms, relieved.

"Hey," Tess said with a big smile. "Nice to see you too."

"What? I mean, how? And, where?" Henry stammered, pointing first at Tess, then at the river, then at nowhere in particular.

Tess angled her baton down another trail, which led to the junction where Henry stood. "From somewhere over there," she said as she walked out of the grass and dug around in the messenger bag slung across her shoulder. She pulled out a tattered, ancient-looking book and held it forward for him to see. The title read, *Your Essential Guide to Star Recovery*. "This helped too."

"But—" Henry began.

"It started with Cassandra," Tess said, anticipating his next question.

"Oh. Ugh," said Henry, looking at Tess with sympathy. Cassandra was the most popular girl in their class. She was also the meanest. How a person could be mean and popular was a mystery to Henry, but Cassandra proved it could be done.

"This is a new baton," Tess said. "She took my old one, whacked me in the arm really hard with it, and then threw it in the lake behind school."

Henry glanced at Tess's arm. He saw a harsh purplish bruise peeking out from the edge of the sleeve of her blouse.

Tess continued, "I cried all the way home. Then, when I got to my room, a big star shot right out of my ear. It was the first one I'd ever seen, and it hurt so much I swear I thought part of my brain had popped out." Tess rubbed her ear as if the whole episode were still hurting her.

"Why is Cassandra so mean?" Henry said.

"I have *no* idea. My mom says happy people don't act that way, and I should feel sorry for her," Tess said with a huff. "Fat chance! Anyway, what about you? How'd you get here?"

"I broke the snow globe in our hallway and lied about it."

"The big one with the geese and goats?"

"They're rams. Yeah," Henry said.

"I loooved that one," she said, her smile dissolving. "It was the coolest and prettiest ever."

"Yeah," Henry said, furrowing his forehead and kicking the dirt. "My mom loved it too."

Tess pursed her lips as if she understood exactly how that made Henry feel, but a very wet *squish-squash* behind them interrupted their conversation. Turning, they watched as Henry's leaf squeezed itself back to its normal size.

"Whoa, cool," Tess said as Henry bent down to reattach his jump rope. "Didn't your parents bring you that from Costa Rica?"

"Yeah."

"I remember when you brought it to show-and-tell last year and everybody made fun of you at recess and said it was lame and that your mom and dad were lame for bringing back such a lame gift."

"Thanks for the reminder," Henry said, looking at the ground. He pretended he was focused on the knot he was tying instead of remembering that day.

What Henry's classmates saw as lame, he saw as exotic, almost alien, something that could have come from outer space or the middle of the earth just as easily as from another country. That's why he kept it tacked to his wall.

"I didn't think it was lame," Tess said. "I thought it was super cool. I didn't know leaves got that big. I mean, I'd seen them on TV and everything, but they didn't look *that* big. It was almost like an alien or something."

Henry looked up at Tess and smiled. "It *is* pretty great," he said. "I would have drowned without it." In fact, as he flung the leaf back over his shoulder and ran his hand down its edge, he thought it was pretty much the greatest gift his parent's had ever given him. When was the last time a video game had saved his life? Never, that's when!

He nodded towards the wooden sign. "So, uh, I guess I'm supposed to go that way now." He was unsure of where Tess was headed. "What about you...?"

Henry flinched. The sign now said: "*THIS WAY, HENRY AND TESS!*"

"Same as you, Mr. Kung-Fu," Tess said, giggling and beginning to walk. "I'm a poet and I don't know it."

"Ugh," Henry said, shaking his head and grimacing as if that were the worst rhyme he'd ever heard, which reminded him of Lion, which reminded him of how Lion had said there were no zorkalorks to worry about. He made a mental note to tell that cat how terribly wrong she'd been. That was, if he somehow managed not to get eaten by a zorkalork, somehow managed to collect his stars, and somehow managed to figure out how to get home. All of which made him queasy.

"Hold on."

Scrambling to the top of the nearest, biggest boulder, he shielded his eyes from the sun's white light with his hands and scanned the horizon. He saw no zorkalorks or three-legged gobblygoks or headless bogeymen or anything of that sort. He drew a sharp breath through his nose. He did not smell the hairy beasts' tuna casserole stench. He jumped down from the boulder and bumped casually into Tess. "OK. Let's go."

Tess nodded and said, "Let's go."

***

The dusty trail rolled through the wildflower-spiked meadow, and then dove into a forest that smelled like vanilla and apricots. As they entered the forest, Tess began to recount what had happened once she'd found *Your Essential Guide to Star Recovery*. The guidebook, she said, had told her how people lost stars, and how, if she wanted her stars back, the first thing she had to do was touch the big spider web in the corner of her closet. "And I'd rather lick dirt than do that. Spiders, bleh," she said, her whole body shuddering.

Squirrels and beavers and deer stopped their gnawing and chewing to watch them walk past. Henry swore they were whispering to each other and pointing their paws and hooves at them.

Tess stopped walking to recount what had happened next. "When I finally got up the nerve to touch it, this jumbo-mumbo spider sprang out of my dollhouse, and the next thing I knew, I woke up inside a cocoon."

"*No way,*" Henry said.

She held up her baton. "I had to bash my way out of there, and when I fell out, I hit the ground in this place." She held up her elbow so he could see the red-black-blue spot where she'd landed.

"Ouch," Henry said.

They were rock-hopping across a stream that sparkled like diamonds and plink-plink-plinked as it rippled over glistening pink and red rocks.

"You know what else is weird?" Henry said. "This river sounds like the music box on my mom's dresser. I think she said it was 'Bridge Over Troubled Waters' by some group called Simon and Garfield."

53

"Garfunkel," said Tess.

"Huh?"

"It's Simon & Garfunkel. My brother has one of their albums."

"Oh, right. Ha," Henry said. "All I know is Mom hugs me and cries every time she hears it. She says they're 'happy tears,' whatever that means."

Henry sighed and looked up. Above him, a group of eagles appeared to be playing a game of aerial tag.

"I kind of wish she could be here right now," he said.

Tess said, "Totally. I wish my brother could be here too."

Across the stream, they entered another forest, this one with trees that had bark made of purple velour and bushes with red corduroy leaves.

"How'd *you* get here?" Tess asked, petting a corduroy bush.

"Wait a sec," Henry said, stopping and holding his hand up. Tess froze. The leaf under her hand arched like a dog wanting its back scratched. "Do you hear buzzing?" Henry said. It sounded like the drone of planes that were far off but closing in quickly. They turned to look behind them.

A swarm of bugs, iridescent orange with lightning bolts of blue down their wings, was bulleting straight towards them. Each had two heads and was as big as Henry's forearm. Worst of all, jutting from each face was a proboscis like a knitting needle.

"Run!" they both yelled.

Bolting down the path, Henry glanced over his shoulder and stumbled over a rock. One of the monster bugs shot over his head. It slammed into a nearby tree, and its proboscises sank deep into the soft purple bark, stuck. "Holy moly cannoli!" Henry exclaimed, scrabbling along on his hands and feet until he regained his balance.

Once he was back on his feet, Tess shot past him, her hair floating out behind her just as in the schoolyard. But this time there was a flying demon in hot pursuit. It appeared to be so eager to entangle itself in her auburn

54

locks that it was ignoring Henry altogether. He swatted it hard with the back of his hand. It veered into a wild tailspin, smashing into one of the red corduroy bushes in an explosion of leaves.

"Over there!" Tess yelled, pointing to a lake up ahead off the side of the trail. Sprinting, they dove in.

The water was lukewarm, like a bath. Tess instantly disappeared into it, but Henry's leaf sprang to its full size the moment it touched the water, pinning him to the surface. In a panic, he tried to get ride of it by throwing the jump rope up over his head, but instead he thoroughly entangled his arms.

"Eeiiiiiii!" Henry screamed, his eyes widening at the sight of the flying knitting needles bearing down on him.

They were mere inches from his face when he felt Tess's hands wrap around his ankle.

Yank!

Henry dropped below the surface fast and deep. The bugs, unable to pull up, began to *plip*, *plop*, and *ploop* into the water all around them.

The plipping and plopping kept plooping and plipping until Henry felt his chest tighten. He was running out of air. He looked at Tess, her hair flowing wild in the water like red seaweed, and pointed towards the surface. She shook her head no even though her face was turning purple. He shook his head yes! and began pulling her up.

They rose slowly, their remaining bubbles of air escaping and billowing up around them as the last bugs kamikazed into the lake.

"That was *way* too close!" Henry exclaimed with a gasp as he broke the water's surface.

Tess took a huge gasp of air and giggled, "Your face would have looked like a golf ball if I hadn't pulled you down!"

"Or a bag of marbles," Henry countered, jubilant that he'd escaped.

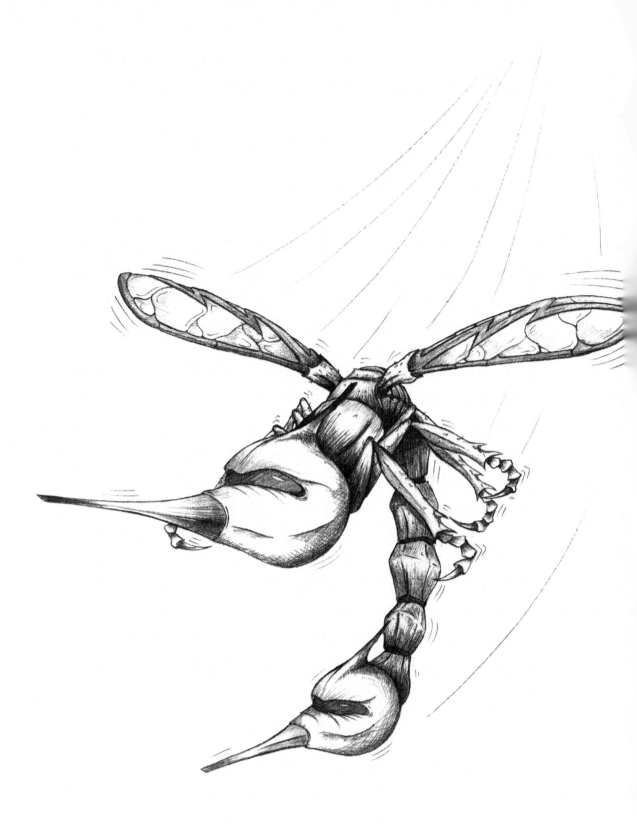

"Or moldy Swiss cheese," Tess said.

"Or zombie brains," Henry laughed as they reached the shore and walked out of the water.

Down the beach, some of the bugs were spiking their wings into the sand and, with great strain, pulling themselves out of the water, flopping onto their back, and making panting and buzzing sounds. They looked waterlogged and exhausted, as if they'd just swum the English Channel, and when one sneezed, a blue-black broth shot out the end of its needle.

"Big black bugs bleed blue-black blood, but baby black bugs bleed blue blood," Henry said with deliberate slowness.

"What?" Tess said.

"Try saying that ten times fast. Bet you can't even do it once."

"But they're orange, silly."

"I *know* they're orange, but 'Big orange bugs bleed blue-orange blood, but baby orange bugs bleed blue blood' isn't as hard to say."

Tess squeezed one eye shut and appeared to be running through both versions in her head. "You're right," she said.

"Told you," Henry said, picking up his leaf. It'd shrunk back to its normal size.

Hitting the trail again, they took turns seeing who could rat-a-tat-tat the tongue twister faster. One of them would attempt saying it while the other quietly counted: One hippopotamus, two hippopotamus, three hippopotamus...

Henry won by half a hippopotamus and shot his fists into the sky, victorious.

Tess rolled her eyes. "Whatever."

Henry felt the heat of the afternoon sun working its way through his wet T-shirt. He wondered what this place would be like when the sun went down.

"Hey, you *still* haven't told me how you got here," Tess said.

"Oh, right. It was completely, absolutely, positively nuts," he said, and he began telling Tess how he'd crawled under his bed and fallen through the floor. He was just getting to the part about fighting the zorkalorks when a gaggle of butterflies waltzed past them, each one dancing with a floathing flame of fire. "No way! Check those out," Henry said, pointing. "That is so cool!"

"Thanks," Tess said with a glint in her eye, bobbing her head.

"Huh?"

Tess pulled *Your Essential Guide to Star Recovery* out of her messenger bag; water drained from its soggy, droopy pages as she began gently leafing through it. When she found the page she was looking for, she showed it to Henry. There was a drawing of a girl, who looked suspiciously like Tess, aiming a knobbly stick at a pair of zorkalorks. "I just twirl my baton and say, 'Zorkalork, shmorkalork, mean and lame. Dance like a butterfly and a flame.'"

"No way! They tried eating you too?" Henry said.

"Totally. They kept popping out of the woods before I ran into you. That's why I was hiding in the field. I mean, I was resting too because outsmarting all those zorkalorks is pretty freaking exhausting." Henry nodded in agreement. "But mostly I was hiding." She paused and gave Henry a quizzical look as she closed the book with a wet *thlurp*. "But you don't have a baton or a magic wand or anything like that. How'd you not get eaten?"

"By blowing at them."

"Blowing? Like *phew-phew*?" Tess said, raising her eyebrows and blowing as if trying to cool a spoonful of hot soup.

"Yeah, I know. I didn't think it'd work either," Henry said, and he reenacted how he'd sent the zorkalorks flying. "I had to blow a lot harder than that and make this sound like a siren—*ZEEEEWWWW*. Then they'd fly across the cave, slam into the wall, and get knocked out cold."

"Cool!" Tess said.

"And then," Henry said, reaching into his pocket and pulling out the flashlight, "I bonked this extra-extra-large, really, really mean one on the head with this."

"Dang," Tess said, sounding impressed. They stopped at a split in the trail. They'd already passed through a number of junctions and had discovered that all they had to do was be patient and wait: Soon enough, a flower or a rotting log or a pile of rocks would begin to quiver, and a wooden sign would shoot up emblazoned with the words: *"THIS WAY, HENRY AND TESS!"*

This time a particularly pitiful, slumped-over sign soon sprouted out of the dark-purple knothole in a nearby tree. The sign pointed down the trail to their left.

"Thanks," Henry said without thinking, then glanced at Tess, feeling embarrassed. He'd just thanked a piece of wood as if it were a person. True, this particular piece of wood looked to be in dire need of appreciation, but it was still only a piece of wood.

"Don't mention it," the sign said in a guff voice, perking up. Henry and Tess looked at each other for a moment, then burst out laughing.

"Yeah, thanks a lot," Tess said, smiling.

"Don't mention it," said the sign.

"Totally," said Henry, wanting to keep the game going. "Really, thanks a bunch."

"Yes, yes. You're welcome."

"Seriously. It really means a *lot*," Tess said, winking at Henry. "Thanks."

"All right! Enough already," the sign said. "Move along."

Giggling, they did as they were told.

After three more junctions, each marked by a wooden sign that barked, "Don't mention it" or "You're welcome" in response to being thanked, Henry and Tess began picking their way through a vast rock garden. Rocks of all sizes lay jammed against each other. Boulders as big as cars balanced on stones no bigger than Henry's fist. Between the rocks were cracks and holes that looked perfect for snapping an ankle.

"Careful," Henry said.

"Definitely," said Tess as she began hopscotching from one rock to the next.

Crrrack!

They froze. Tess was wobbling on one leg like a drunk flamingo, and Henry was crouched on a rock nearby with one leg up like a dog. It'd sounded as if a thick branch had broken off a tree deep in the woods, or—Henry's mind whirled—one had been stepped on by a nappy, stinky, razor-clawed foot. He peered into the maze of purple branches and corduroy leaves behind him. A faint stench tickled his nose.

"Who's there?!" he said. His voice quivered. Tess wrapped her hand around the baton sticking out of her bag. A twittering of birds was the only answer Henry received.

Henry took a long breath through his nose but now he only caught the vanilla-apricot aroma of the woods.

"Probably just a branch breaking off a tree," he said at last.

"Or a rabbit or something," said Tess warily, and they began picking their way through the rocks again.

Henry muttered, "That'd have to be a pretty big rabbit."

"Hey!" Tess countered. "This place has bushes with corduroy leaves, and creeks that sound like music boxes. Maybe it has really big rabbits too, OK?" It was the first time Henry could hear any fear in her voice.

"OK, OK," he said.

They were halfway across the rock field when a whistlelike shriek—*Screeeeeee!*—brought them to a standstill again.

It sounded like a teapot boiling—clearly not a zorkalork—and was coming from somewhere beneath the rocks. They looked at each other, worried. Henry took a cautious step forward, and a jet of super-hot steam shot up through a crack where he'd been standing, a hair shy of scalding his butt.

"Uh-oh," they said in unison as what sounded like a teapot orchestra began punctuating the air. They sprang into action hopscotching across the boulders at double speed. The rock garden fired jets of scorching steam to their left, to their right, in front of them, all around them. Henry was bobbing and weaving like a football player avoiding tackles, amazing even himself.

Hurtling a boulder, he landed on all fours, glanced down, and saw a patch of fluorescent-green and brown moss just below his stomach. It was covered with tooth-filled orange openings and made a sliggering, gurgling noise as it lunged at him from its perch on a rock. His eyes bulged. *Man-eating moss!* He spun left, but not fast enough.

The moss ripped itself from the rock and latched onto his shirt. Its teeth, just long enough to poke through the fabric, nipped at him like hundreds of sharp pinches, shredding their way through the shirt. "Eee-yaaa!" Henry yelped, ripping off the section of shirt where the moss clung.

"Henry!" Tess cried. She'd cleared the rock field and was standing safely on the dirt trail beyond it.

Henry spun the tattered fabric around like a lasso, faster and faster, until the moss lost its hold. It flew across the rock field, taking bits of the shirt with it, and smacked into a jet of scorching vapor. It made a horrible screeching noise, like nails being drawn down a chalkboard, and fell, boiled black, to the ground. It flopped once, let loose another terrible screech, withered, and ceased to move.

Henry bolted for the edge of the rock garden, diving onto the dirt trail as a geyser of vapor blew up under his feet.

"Holy cannoli," he said, looking up at Tess, his chest heaving.

He was lying on his back with his arms and legs splayed out, shocked to be alive.

Looking at him with a big smile, Tess pulled the baton from her bag and tapped him on the shoulders. "I officially dub thee Sir Henry Cornwall of Zigzaggedness and Nimble Feet."

"I can't believe I didn't eat it. Or get eaten!" Henry said, and cleared his throat to play along with Tess. "My thanks to thee for that most noble title," he said as he took the baton from her and touched her knees with it. "And to thee I grant the title Lady Tess of Swiftdomness and Most Premium Ankle-Pullingitude."

Tess gave a graceful bow and helped pull Henry to his feet.

"Onward!" Henry said, holding the baton up to the sky and then handing it back to Tess.

"Onward!" she said, and she too thrust it towards the sky.

Chapter 11

They didn't get far before they came to a giant white oak tree near the edge of a deep canyon. Across the canyon, Henry could see the trail continuing up the mountain that had been growing bigger on the horizon all day. What he couldn't see was any way to get across. Looking down, all he could see was a reddish-black mist hanging far, far below.

Henry sat beneath the tree, splayed his legs, and propped his arms behind him. Tess plopped down cross-legged next to him. They looked towards the opposite side of the canyon.

"Got any ideas?" Henry asked.

"Nope."

The late-day sun was reflecting off the mountain in a kaleidoscope of yellows and oranges, casting long shadows over the canyon walls, which oozed red dirt and mud, reminding Henry of the blood that had gushed down Tess's leg after he'd pushed her.

"Shoot," he mumbled softly. He considered apologizing.

"What?" Tess said.

"Uh, nothing." He didn't want to remind Tess about that day. She might get mad at him.

Tess gave Henry a questioning look but then said, "Okaaay. Anyway, so how in the heck are we going to get across?"

Henry mumbled, "Looks impossible," but a gust of wind cut through the canyon, drowning out his words. The wind siphoning through the crevasse sounded like a ghost in an empty gymnasium, moaning from a bellyache. Henry made his best spooky noise: "Ooooooooh."

"Stop it," Tess said.

"Scared?"

"No."

"Are too," Henry said, a little scared himself.

"Am not."

"Are too."

"You're going to lose a star if you don't watch it," Tess said.

Henry shut his mouth.

He didn't like the feel of this place one bit, what with the teapot rock garden and moaning winds and possible giant rabbits. He wanted to keep moving, pronto. As he leaned forward to get a better look into the canyon, the sharp point of his pencil poked him in the leg.

"I think I've got an idea," he said.

Tess looked over and watched Henry pull the pencil out of his pocket.

"What in the world are you going to do with that?" Tess asked, looking at him as if he'd just pulled out a badger.

Before Henry could answer, another branch cracked behind them, this one near the tree line. They sprang up and spun around. Henry sucked in a deep lungful of air and felt the hair on the back of his neck stand on end. Tess poised her baton like a sword.

"Show yourself," Henry stammered.

"Are you crazy?" hissed Tess.

"Uh," she yelled into the woods, "you don't have to show yourself if you don't want to. It's cool."

There was a skittering sound, and a rabbit popped onto the trail almost as if it'd been pushed. The rabbit was five times as big as a standard household rabbit. It looked behind itself, stuck out its tongue, and bolted in a wide arc back into the woods.

"Told you," Tess declared, putting her baton back in her bag and shaking her head from side to side. "This place is going to drive me batty."

"Nah," Henry said, trying to sound braver than he felt. "Even if there were a zorkalork around—not that there is, 'cause there's not—it'd be no match for us, not with your baton and my siren of air and all." He began to untie the jump rope from the leaf and secure one end of it to the pencil's eraser.

"Maybe," Tess said, unsure.

Henry tied the other end to a low sturdy branch on the oak tree.

"So, really, what're you going to do with all that?" Tess asked again.

Henry held the pencil above his head like a javelin. "This!" he said, and he began taking long, leaping strides towards the edge of the canyon. He counted, "One! Two! Thre—," but broke his stride to avoid tripping on a gnarled root sticking out of the ground.

"Ha! Not this time!" he exclaimed. The scene of him tripping on the root in the schoolyard played in his head. "For I am Sir Henry Cornwall of Zigzaggedness and Nimble Feet!"

"Oh brother," Tess said, rolling her eyes.

He restarted his approach, focusing even harder on the far side of the canyon, counting even louder.

"One. Two..."

He came up to the rim of the canyon, lunged forward, and—"Three!"— hurled the pencil towards the far side. As he'd hoped, the pencil grew into a long yellow spear the moment it left his hand. The jump rope, meanwhile, stretched like an enormous rubber band. When the pencil hit the far edge of the canyon, it dug itself deep into the ground with a loud thud.

"Awesome!" Henry cried, pumping his fists.

Tess's jaw dropped. "That was super cool," she said.

Henry tugged the rope. It was taut and secure. He climbed atop of the line, holding the tree for balance with one hand and gripping the leaf with the other.

"You're going to walk across?" Tess said. Her eyes widened as she looked from Henry into the canyon.

"Of course," Henry said. He puffed up his chest and declared, "For I am Sir Henry Cornwall of Zigzag—"

Tess held up a hand. "OK, OK. I know. I came up with the name, remember?"

Henry stuck out his tongue and crossed his eyes. He felt giddy and confident. He was sure he was about to make his way across as easily as a circus tightrope walker. He let go of the tree and took a step. The line wobbled and almost threw him, but he regained his balance. His face lit up.

He took another step. The line swung hard to the right, and Henry bounced off the rope and slammed into the ground.

"Ow," Henry said, squeezing his eyes shut and trying to shake off the pain. "That hurt. That hurt. That. Hurt."

He heard Tess snickering. She had her hands covering her mouth.

"Oh yeah, ostri—" Henry said before shutting his mouth tight.

Tess interrupted her giggle with a loud abrupt snort and quickly said, "Sorry. I mean sorry I laughed. Sorry. Sorry. Sorry. That was mean."

They looked at each other, and Henry waited for a star to pop out of one of them. But once it was clear neither of them was going to lose a star, they cracked up.

"That snort was awesome," Henry said.

"So was the way you bounced off the rope, Sir Nimblefeet," Tess said, giggling and walking over to the rope.

"Yeah. I've had a lot of practice falling and bouncing off things." Henry sounded much humbler than he had standing on top of the rope. "I thought one of us was going to lose a star there for sure."

Tess crouched and grabbed the line with both hands.

"My book says that if you apologize in time you won't lose one."

She swung her ankles over the rope. Hanging underneath, she looked at Henry and said, "You must have caught yourself in time before you finished calling me an ostrich. So you didn't lose one either." With that she shimmied her way over the crevasse.

Henry said, "You look like an orangutan."

He grimaced as soon as the words had left his mouth. He didn't want his stars to misinterpret that remark. Looking at the sky and raising his arms, he said, "And I mean that as a compliment!"

"Thanks. It's easy," Tess said just as her hands slipped off the rope.

Her scream was wild and terror-filled.

"Tess!"

Henry reached towards her as if it would prevent her from falling, but it was her feet criss-crossed over the rope that saved her. She looked down and swallowed.

"It's OK. I'm OK," she gasped, and she began to swing her arms back and forth, back and forth. With each swing, her hands reached a little higher, until she was able to grab the rope. Quickly she scampered to the other side and dropped to the ground.

"Your turn," she yelled, panting.

"*Great*," Henry said with mock enthusiasm.

Clasping the leaf between his teeth, Henry made his way over the void. The words *Got...to...be...brave...Got...to...be...brave* tumbled through his brain. He was halfway across when the wind moaned through the canyon again.

Except, Henry realized, he didn't feel any wind.

"It hurts," a voice whispered. It sounded like someone stepping on a creaky wooden floor.

Henry almost lost his grip on the rope. He looked to his left and to his right and down past his feet. Nothing. He bent his head all the way back to look at Tess. She shrugged and said, "Wasn't me."

"The bleeding. Make it stop," the voice said, pleading.

Henry looked into the bottomless canyon and its oozing red walls. Tess's bloody knee flashed through his head again. The walls, he realized. The walls were bleeding.

"*No way*," Henry said.

He shimmied across the rest of the rope as fast as he could, and dropped down next to Tess.

"It's the canyon," Henry said to Tess, taking the leaf from his mouth.

"Huh?" said Tess.

"The canyon. It's bleeding."

"Nuh-uh."

"Yuh-huh," Henry said. They got on their hands and knees and looked into the misty void.

The canyon began to howl and sob: "It hurts so bad. Make it stop. Please, make it stop."

"Oh, jeesh," Tess said, turning to look at Henry. She bit her lower lip.

"Well?"

"Well, what?"

"Well, what do you think we should do?"

"I have completely, absolutely, positively no clue," Henry said. Looking into the mist, he called out, "We...we don't know what to do. We're only kids."

"But I'm a half year older," Tess announced, sitting up on her knees.
Henry rolled his eyes.

"Can we stick to the problem here?" Henry said, pointing into the canyon.

"Oh, um, yeah. Sorry," said Tess.

"Pleeease," pleaded the canyon.

Henry felt tears welling from somewhere deep inside. He wanted to help. He wished he could make the pain go away as his Mom did for him. Whenever he hurt himself, she'd bandage him up, plop a big bag of ice onto the injury, and, most importantly, give him a long warm hug while stroking his hair. That helped erase the pain every time. Here, though, it would take a gigantic bandage and an avalanche of ice. A hug was out of the question, and there was no hair to stroke. He had completely, absolutely, positively no clue what to do.

"We, um, we'll go get help," Henry said.

Tess looked at Henry with a scrunched-up face and cupped her hands around his ear. "There's no one else around here but kamikaze bugs and giant rabbits," she whispered. "Who's going to help us?"

Henry gritted his teeth and shrugged. He went to his jump rope and gave it three quick jerks. He'd tied it around the white oak with a special knot his dad had taught him. It was supposed to release when you gave it three sharp tugs, but the rope didn't free itself. Instead the far side of the canyon slid three inches closer to Henry.

"That's better," the canyon gasped. "Keep pulling."

"*No way*," they said, shocked.

"Tess, c'mon. Help me!"

They began pulling as hard and fast as they could. Soon they were huffing and puffing, and Henry felt his heart pounding like a jackhammer, but, inch by inch, the two sides of the canyon were coming together.

Three hundred and four pulls later, the canyon sealed together with a large hiss of air. The ground was ecstatic. "That's it!" the ground exclaimed.

"I thank you both a thousand times over...but, my boy, whatever happened to your shirt?"

Henry looked down at his shirt, his chest heaving for air. "Man-eating moss," he spat out between breaths.

"Really?" the ground said. "Well, we're both lucky you survived that one."

Henry nodded in agreement. "But how'd this happen?" he gasped.

"Yeah, how'd you crack open?" Tess echoed.

The ground gently rose and fell beneath their feet as if it were sighing. "Oh, it's just something I do. A bad habit, really. Things make me mad, like when zorkalorks spray me with puckicide."

"Puckicide?" Henry said between breaths.

Tess crinkled her nose as if she'd just smelled a bucket full of rotten eggs.

"Yes," the canyon said. "They spray it all over the place to kill all the flowers and corduroy bushes, so more stinkweed will grow for their stink weed tea."

"Puuuucky," Tess said.

"Exactly," the ground said. "Makes them smell something awful too."

"Yeah, like my mom's tuna casserole," Henry said.

"Ew, yeah, totally," Tess said. She'd been over to Henry's house for dinner and had the misfortune of being served his mom's casserole.

"Or," the canyon continued, "I'll get mad because a comet comes crashing down and punches me from outer space, which can really, really hurt! Or the zorkalorks throw trash all over the place. Stuff like that. And I keep all that angry and painful stuff jammed down deep inside when I should let it out. Until, one day, whammo, something sets me off and I scream and I quake and I shake and I crack. This time it was because a horde of those kamikaze bugs had stuck their needles into me and tried to suck my blood. Those things freaking hurt!"

"Ow," Henry said.

"But I always wish I hadn't afterwards. I always wish I'd let it all out in little bits and tremors instead of letting it build up. But noooo. I end up splitting myself open like a dry old piece of leather, bleeding all over the place and making it even easier for those bugs to get their fill. They are always *sooo* proud of themselves when they make me explode and I crack open. Anyway, then I have to wait until someone like you comes along and figures out how to get me back together. Yours was a most innovative approach, by the way, although I'm not sure the part where you bounced off the rope and slammed into me was necessary."

"Me neither," Henry said, lying down. He was still trying to catch his breath. Tess, who was also breathing hard, set her bag on the ground and sat next to him.

"And let me tell you," said the ground, "it can take years before someone figures out how to get me back together. Not to mention—"

The ground paused, then began vibrating: "Zorkalork! Ten o'clock! Zorkalork. Ten o'clock!"

Tess stiffened and Henry bolted upright. His eyes grew to the size of ping-pong balls as Spike charged out from the trees.

Henry tried to take a deep breath, but the best he could do was gasp and let out a meek-sounding "zeee." He had no breath left. Tess grabbed for her bag with such force that her baton popped out and rolled beyond her reach. Henry tried scooting back up the trail, only to fall over himself. Tess looked frozen with fear.

Spike bellowed:

Ook-ah-ew!
Cookies and tea!
Now me got you—
me eat Tess 'n' Henry!

Chapter 12

Spike pounced on them, pinning Tess to the ground with a big, meaty paw while slamming his knee onto Henry's stomach. There was no way Henry could take a deep breath now. The monster brought his big ugly tooth-filled face within an inch of Henry's. Goop dripped off his nose hair onto Henry's face. It was all Henry could do not to gag on his foul, rotten tuna breath.

The monster's toady voice bore into Henry as he pressed a claw into his chest. "Me follow Henry 'n' Tess. Me wait 'til Henry 'n' Tess all pooped. Me trick Henry 'n' Tess and push rabbit on trail."

Spike sounded very proud of himself. Henry winced as a spot of blood began soaking through his T-shirt from under Spike's claw.

"Me thought Henry 'n' Tess escape over canyon, but Henry pull me back. Ha ha ha ha ha ha ha ha."

Henry felt the monster's crazed laugh in his bones. Spike raised his paw high, ready to strike. The claws glinted in the sun.

"Me kill Henry 'n' Tess now! Eat with cookies and tea!"

Henry squeezed his eyes shut and waited for Spike's claws to strike. He wondered whether he would die the moment Spike struck him or if it would be long and painful. Behind his closed eyelids the image of his parents popped up. They were standing in the doorway of his bedroom after he'd broken the snow globe. They weren't upset this time, though. They were looking at him with love in their eyes.

"Mom. Dad," he whispered.

"Leave them alone!" the ground demanded, rumbling and shaking, trying to throw Spike off Henry and Tess without success.

"Henry," Tess whimpered, her voice full of desperation and fear. Henry assumed Spike's paw was now swinging towards him.

ZEEEEWWWW!

A gigantic gust of air rushed past them, and Spike's weight vanished from Henry's stomach. A coarse roar filled the air: *"Noooooooooo!"*

Henry opened one eye and then the other as the ground stopped shaking. Spike was flying back, back, back in the direction of the zorkalorks' cave. Henry and Tess slowly turned around.

"No way," Henry said.

A humongous bear stood behind them wearing a white bathrobe and a patch on one eye. The bear was chomping on blue chewing gum, chuckling and twirling his thumbs. He appeared to be thoroughly enjoying the sight of Spike disappearing over the horizon.

"Ray!" the ground exclaimed. Its voice was one of relief edged with annoyance. "Once again, right in the nick of time."

"Hey there," the bear said, holding up a furry paw in greeting. "Sorry. I was deep into my weekly grooming session, and my blow dryer blew a gasket last month. Now it's louder than a freight train, and I didn't hear all the ruckus 'til I was breaking out the styling gel, which, by the way, and lucky for you, I skipped. Another second and you would have been a zorkalork shish kebab."

He blew an enormous blue bubble. When it was bigger than his head,

it broke, and the bear peeled it from his fur, leaving blue specks behind. Henry thought that if the bear kept that up, his face would be completely blue by the next grooming session.

"Like the ground said, the name's Ray. And, *whew*, is it just me or did that zorkalork stink like a poopsicle?" Ray pinched his nose and fanned himself with his big floppy paw.

"You can say that again," Tess said.

"Is it just me or did that zorkalork stink like a poopsicle?" the bear said.

Henry traded a questioning look with Tess, not sure what to make of Ray.

"Uh, right," Henry said, standing up and dusting the dirt off the back of his shorts. "I'm Sir Henry Cornwall of Zigzaggedness and Nimble Feet, and this is Lady Tess of Swiftdomness and Most Premium Ankle-Pullingitude." He rolled a hand in Tess's direction.

"The who-be-da-dobbie-de-whobody-who? And the what-ditty-what-ditty-what-ditty-what?" Ray said.

"Just call me Tess." Tess stood and walked forward to shake Ray's paw. "And that's Henry. Nice to meet you. I didn't really mean you should say all that about the zorkalork stinking like a poopsicle again, though."

"Oh," said Ray, chuckling but not embarrassed. "My bad."

"Man, you totally saved us," Henry said.

"*No problemo*. I mean, those zorkalorks and I..." The bear stopped, nodded towards Henry's shirt, and said, "What happened there, little man? Got moths in the closet? Have a run-in with a weed whacker? Punk making a comeback? That's what it is, isn't it? Punk is making a comeback. I swear, we're always like six months behind on what's new and cool on the fashion front."

"Man-eating moss," Henry said as he pulled his pencil out of the ground with both hands and watched it shrink to its original size.

"No kidding? And you're still breathing? Wish I could have seen that. Anywho, as I was saying, those zorkalorks and I have a long history," the bear said, pointing at his eye patch. "And I love sending them flying—zorka-lork airmail, so to speak. I'll tell you what, though. Hitting that cave wall is going to hurt something awful from this far out. I almost feel sorry for the big stinko." Ray laughed again and fluttered his fingers in the direction Spike had disappeared. "Almost."

The bear spun around and threw a paw in the direction of the sign behind him that said: *"THIS WAY, HENRY AND TESS!"*

"All righty," Ray said. "My keen bear instincts tell me you are going this way up the mountain. Probably to get your stars back, huh?"

"Right," Tess said.

"C'mon then, we've got a lot of ground to cover." Ray paused and looked at the sun sitting low on the horizon. "And not much time."

"How'd you know about our stars?" Henry said, untying his rope from the tree and grabbing the leaf off the ground.

"That what folks come here for," Ray said very matter-of-factly. "Now, c'mon, enough questions. We've got to get moving."

"But can't we rest some first? We're really tired," Henry said, making his body look limp and exhausted.

"Yeah," Tess agreed.

"Nope. No way. Not an option."

"Why?" they both said with a whine in their voices.

"Seriously? Ah, OK, c'mon then, climb up on my back. Let's go. Hup, hup."

"Awesome," they said in unison, giving each other a high five before climbing atop Ray.

"Your fur's super-soft," Tess said. "Like feathers."

"Thanks," said Ray, holding his head a bit higher and looking very proud of his fur. "I use this really great organic conditioner. It's formulated especially for extra-dry bear hair. It costs a little more, but let me tell you, it's absolutely worth it. The sows can't keep their paws off it."

"Sows?" Henry said, interrupting.

"Female bears, little man. Female bears."

"Oh, right," Henry said, wondering whether sows had cooties too. "But I still don't get it. What's the rush? And why are you helping us?"

The ground interrupted, "Trust Ray, and hurry."

Ray replied, "Helping is just what I do—wish more creatures did the same, actually—but don't get me started. There's no time for rhapsodizing. Sun's going down. Moon is going to start rising. We've got to get moving. So close your traps and hang on."

"Good luck," said the ground.

"Thanks," Henry said as he and Tess waved, but his voice was lost in the thunder and dust of Ray galloping up the trail.

The mountain was taller than any Henry had ever seen in a magazine or on TV or the time he and his parents had driven through the Rocky Mountains in Colorado. The higher the trail got, the narrower and windier it became, causing Ray to run into an increasing number of tree branches, fallen logs, and rocks.

After he slammed into a particularly large branch that almost knocked Henry and Tess off his back, Ray yelled, "Sorry for the rough ride back there. It's this bad eye. The ol' depth perception is completely out of whack."

Henry grabbed Ray's head. "How about I steer?"

"And I'll navigate," Tess said, sitting up straighter so she could see farther down the trail.

"Excellent!" the bear chortled.

With Tess calling out, "Left!...Right!...Log coming! Jump!" and Henry doing the driving, they closed in on the mountain's peak just as the moon began to rise.

The moon looked like a cookie that had an enormous bite taken out of it. It was nearing the summit of the mountain when Ray began running faster

than it seemed an animal his size should be able to. A typical grizzly bear can run thirty miles per hour, but Ray was easily doing fifty, making the tail of his white robe flap and *snap!* behind them.

"Yeehaw!" Henry cried, barely able to hear his voice over the roar of wind.

Henry's hair was being blown backwards and becoming plastered to the sides of his head. Now it looked short on the top and short on the sides but long in back.

"You've got a mullet," Tess yelled, giggling.

"A what?" Henry yelled over the wind.

"A mullet. That's what Dad calls it. He says it's all business in the front but rock 'n' roll in the back."

Henry ran a hand through his hair and gave Tess a goofy, cheesy smile, making them crack up as Ray cleared a boulder and almost sent Henry flying again. Grabbing hold of Ray with both hands, he yelled, "Hey! Ray! I still don't get what the big hurry is."

Ray yelled back, "The moon. It's your forklift!"

"Our what?" Henry and Tess cried.

"Your forklift. Your ride to the stars. ¿*Comprende?*"

"Tree!" Tess yelled. Henry jerked Ray's head to the right, missing the fallen tree by inches.

"No. I don't get it," Henry replied much too loudly as Ray slowed down to a saunter. They'd crested the mountain.

Henry looked up over Ray's head as the bear came to a stop. The summit's flat, yellow-brown expanse was bare except for a lone tree, which was old and gnarled, but looked to be thick and strong. The moon was rising behind it.

Chapter 13

Henry and Tess slid off of Ray while staring at the moon. It looked huge and seemed to be ascending just beyond the mountain. Henry said, "It looks like I could jump to it."

"Exactly!" replied Ray, standing up on his rear legs and patting patches of dirt and dust off his robe and fur. "Crud, it's going to take forever for me to get these dirt clumps out of my fur."

"Exactly how do you mean 'exactly'?" Tess said.

Ray hooked his thumb claws into his robe's collar and rocked back on his heels. "It's a cinch. All you got to do is run and jump towards the moon. But you can't flinch. That's the key. You've got to believe you can do it, even if you're as scared as a banana at a monkey picnic. You can't let that stop you. And you've got to do it while the moon and the mountain are this close together."

"A banana can't be scared," Tess said as a matter-of-factly. "It's a fruit."

"Says the girl talking to a bear," said Ray, shooting his eyebrows up and down.

Tess considered that for a moment, then nodded. "Good point."

Henry was skeptical about Ray's advice, and shook his head from side to side. "Tess, what does your book say?"

Tess pulled the book from her bag, but as she did, the back half slurped out from between the covers and hit the ground with a wet *plop!*

They all looked at the soggy white blob for a moment before Tess exclaimed, "Shoot! We should have let it dry out after the lake!"

"Ah man," Henry said, kneeling and trying to pick the pages apart. He succeeded only in turning every page he touched into a white mush, except the very top of one page. He held it to the moonlight. The title "10 Highly Desirable Tips to Achieving Ideal Moon Access" was written across it.

Henry brought the fragment close to his face. Under the title, the first sentence began, "There are a variety of ways to access the moon, the most dangerous of which is..." Below that, the page had been mushified.

"*Great,*" Henry mumbled.

"All right, all right," the bear said at last. "I'm telling you it's *all* about the jump. I've seen it done a hundred times, and speaking of time, we've wasted too much of it already. The moon is not going to wait."

"OK then," Tess said, walking towards the far side of the mountaintop. Her voice sounded solid and decided, but Henry caught her eye and saw in it the same doubt he felt.

"Are you sure this is the best way, Ray?" Henry said as they watched Tess stop at the mountain edge and turn around.

"Yep," Ray said. "Well, actually, I don't know whether it's the *best* way, but it's the only way I know. And it's always worked. Except that one time, I guess. Mmm, yeah, that one didn't turn out so well."

"All right. Here I go!"

"Wait," Henry exclaimed, throwing his hands out towards Tess.

But Tess was already cutting across the mountaintop, her legs and arms pumping faster and faster. Her hair lifted in the breeze and flowed out behind her. Her bag bounced off her back, going every which way. Henry cringed as she reached the opposite edge behind the tree and without any hesitation jumped.

Henry's mouth fell open. Tess was floating up through the air. She seemed to hang for a moment at the top of her arc before landing with a soft exhale in the curve of the moon. She looked back at Henry and Ray, a huge smile was plastered across her face.

"That...was...awesome!" she said. "Like when we jump off the swing set at school, but *way* better."

Without a moment's hesitation, Henry positioned himself in the same spot where Tess had begun her run. He yelled, "Back up and give me some landing room!"

"Red rover, red rover, send Henry right over," Tess yelled. Henry smiled. Red Rover was Tess's favorite game at recess. No matter how many times they called her "Amazon" or "ostrich" or "freak," she always broke through the other team's interlocked hands. Henry didn't always break through, but jumping to the moon looked like a piece of cake by comparison.

He took three running steps, stumbled over a rock, regained his footing, and soon found his stride. Although he was still not as fast as Tess, his legs surprised him. They began moving faster than he'd ever thought they could. He felt as if he were the wind itself or, even better, a cheetah ripping across the African plain. Jumping to the moon *was* going to be a snap.

Henry crossed behind the tree and was about to jump when a sliver of black sky no wider than a finger appeared between the bottom of the moon and the mountain.

"Henry! Stop!" Ray bellowed.

Henry skittered, lost his balance, and fell into a somersault. He came to a halt a mere inch from the edge.

Henry peeked over the rim and yelped. The mountainside dropped straight down into darkness.

"Ray!"

Ray trundled over, grabbed Henry's shirt, and pulled him back from the ledge. The bear said, "It was too late. Too late. I told you the moon was not going to wait." Ray pointed to the widening black space below the moon. "That. That right there. That's why I was rushing to get here."

"What do you mean?" Henry said.

"Once that gap appears, it is too late. It doesn't matter how fast you are. It doesn't matter how high you jump. The pull of the moon, the one that helped Tess float over like a deer, is gone. Dang it. Dang it. Dang it. Dang it," Ray said, hitting his fist against his thigh. "And they only line up this way a few times a year, so..."

"So?" Henry said.

"So I'm afraid you're stuck here until the next time around."

"Stuck?" Henry cried. "No! I've got to get my stars. And...and I want to go home!"

Time seemed to slow down. The next minute felt like an hour.

Tess yelled, "What's wrong? Why didn't you jump?"

"We have a minor situation down here," said Ray. "Hold on a sec."

"A minor situation?" Henry yowled. "You call this a minor situation?!"

Ray, looking over at the gnarled old tree, ignored Henry. "Here we go. Here we go. This might work. Henry, you've got to move fast. No time for mistakes. Get to the top of that tree. Climb as high as you can and grab for the moon. It just might work. Get moving, little man. Go! Go! *Go!*"

Henry shut up and ran to the tree. He began climbing, then stopped, looking at Ray.

"Can you come too?" Henry asked.

Ray's eyes widened, and he pointed at himself.

"Me?" Ray said. "Henry, wow. No one has ever asked me before. That's very cool and thank you. But no. I can't. My job is here. There will be others like you. My job is to get them on the moon, and blow away zorkalorks."

Henry jumped off the tree, ran to Ray and hugged him.

"Thank you."

"You're welcome," said Ray, giving him a true bear hug.

"Now get climbing, little man!"

Henry ran back to the tree and began scrambling up its trunk.

"You're like a squirrel!" Ray said, cheering.

Reaching the two highest limbs, which met in a Y, Henry stood on his tip-toes. The point of the moon was just above him. He stretched as far as his body allowed.

"Got it!" he yelled triumphantly as he hooked his fingers over the point of the moon. The moon picked him up off the tree and continued to rise into the sky. The ground fell away fast beneath his feet. Henry could only enjoy the view for a moment though, before his eyes popped wide with terror.

"I'm slipping!" Henry cried.

"Hang on. You can do it, little man!" Ray yelled, but Ray was grimacing and holding a paw just above his good eye, looking as if he wanted to cover it as fast as possible if necessary.

There was an awful sound—*SKA-SKA-SKA-SKAAALLLIIIDE!*—as Henry's hands scraped down the sides of the moon. He looked at the stars above him. His face contorted. "I tried," he whispered, his voice trailing off as his finger lost contact with the moon.

"Gotcha!" said Tess with a huff, grabbing Henry's wrist with both her hands. Grunting and straining, she hauled him into the curve of the moon, and they collapsed onto its dusty surface.

"Holy moly cannoli! Thank you! Thank you! Thank you!" Henry said, sitting up and hugging her before he remembered the cooties thing and let go.

Tess, trying to catch her breath, smiled and wheezed, *"No problemo."*

They heard Ray yell, "Allllrrrright! That was awesome! Nice work." They looked over the edge and saw Ray waving both paws goodbye and blowing another blue bubble. As they waved back, the bubble popped, and through the film of gum covering his face Ray bellowed, "Good luck! Keep your eyes and ears open and don't fall asleep. At least not until you get your stars."

"OK!" Henry yelled back, giving the bear an earnest salute. "And thanks again for the hand."

Ray laughed and, peeling the bubble off, said, "I think you mean *paw*, little man!"

Henry and Tess waved until Ray's outline blended into the top of the mountain. They kept watching as the mountain's dark form became a black splotch on top of the landscape, and the landscape became a silhouette surrounded by blue-white oceans, and then the planet fell away beneath them like an enormous blue and brown marble.

Henry was transfixed by the view. He didn't notice they were both rising ever so slowly off the moon.

"Henry! We're floating!" Tess screamed, delighted.

Henry looked down and gasped, realizing gravity was losing its hold on them. "Like astronauts!" he said, beaming. "Finally!"

Henry pretended to start swimming, while Tess began pirouetting like a ballerina. Henry thought about how he'd never been able to throw a single complete front flip with a twist on his bed. But now, in just one try, he threw a *triple* front flip with a *triple* twist.

"Yay!" he yelled.

"Nice one," Tess said, spinning like a pinwheel.

Henry floated onto his back, and as he looked out into the vastness of space, his eyes bugged. He flipped over and frantically began swimming back towards the moon.

"Tess, get back to the moon! Get back to the moon! Hurry!"

Henry was kicking his legs like a frog and stroking downward. When he reached the moon, he latched onto a crater and hooked his feet inside it. "Ray said the moon's our ride. We've got to stay with it, at least until we find our stars."

Tess was apparently having too much fun rolling through space. She turned a cartwheel and said, "Don't be such a worrywart. We don't need the moon. We can *fly* to our stars." She stuck her arms out like a bird and dropped into a long arc.

"Tess, look up."

Tess rolled over and began doing a lazy backstroke but froze with one arm sticking straight up. Above her, millions and millions of stars glittered and stretched into the infinite blackness of space. She flipped back over and began diving furiously back towards the moon. "Grab my hand! Grab my hand!" she cried.

Finding their stars among all those pinheads of light would be like trying to find a specific grain of sand in the desert. If Ray was right, the moon was their only chance to reach the right place.

"C'mon! Give me your hand," Tess cried again. Henry had never seen her so flustered. He stretched up until only his toes were hooked underneath the lip of the crater, and interlocked his hands with hers. He didn't let go until he'd pulled her down and she'd secured her feet too.

"Thanks," she gasped. "Wow, yeah. Thanks a ton."

"*No problemo.*" Henry said, happy to have been able to save her as she'd just saved him.

Chapter 14

Once they'd calmed down, Henry and Tess reclined back into the curve of the moon and watched the stars pass, the light from each star washing over their faces before it disappeared below the moon.

"Hey, check that out," Tess said, pointing at a crater beneath them.

Henry looked and saw that the crater went all the way through the moon. It was threaded with a rope, the tail of which dangled far, far below. He said, "No way. The moon is a balloon?"

"The moon's a balloon," Tess echoed, chuckling and shaking her head in disbelief. "Who knew?"

"I bet NASA does," said Henry, pretending to shoot baskets. "My dad says no one has ever landed on the moon. That NASA faked it all on movie sets in Hollywood."

Tess looked at him and squinted. "That's ridiculous."

"I know!" Henry replied, and they started laughing.

As their laughter died down, Henry cleared his throat. "I'm...uh...I'm really sorry I pushed you at school...and for calling you an ugly crawdad."

Tess was silent for a moment and cradled her head in her hands. "It's OK," she said. "I shouldn't have called you snail legs."

Henry nodded. "Can I see your stitches?"

She lifted her leg so he could see the seven black stitches looping through her skin. "There's going to be a super-cool scar there once they take 'em out," she said with an air of excitement.

"Yeah. Totally," Henry said, relieved she wasn't mad.

Tess started to hum to herself, seeming to end the conversation, which was a relief to Henry, because he didn't know what else to say. He recognized the tune as a school cheer and began humming it with her.

★★★

"Do you hear that?" Henry said, sitting up and straining his head forward, listening. They'd stopped humming a while ago and had been silently watching thousands and thousands of stars drift by.

"Uh-huh," Tess said, also sitting up.

The buzz was faint but growing louder, and it was the most beautiful sound Henry had ever heard, as if a choir of flutes and birds and falling snow were singing together. A minute later Henry was able to decipher the words, and he grabbed Tess's arm.

"I think it's our stars," he exclaimed.

And the stars were singing:

Henry and Tess, Henry and Tess,
so very glad you found our address.
Henry and Tess, Henry and Tess,
so very glad you found our address.

Henry and Tess gave each other a double high five.

"Yes!" Henry yelled, pumping his fists in the air.

We've been waiting here so long
singing this long-lost song
Now let the moon go, and fly.
Grab hold of us and pry.

"C'mon! Let's go. Let's go!" said Tess.
They pushed off the moon like two kangaroos, and shot into space.

Henry and Tess, Henry and Tess,
so very glad you found our address.

"Wooohooo," Henry cried, racing towards the singing stars. Next to him Tess was throwing flips and cartwheels.

"Tess, here I am! Here I am!" some of the stars began to chant.

"Henry, over here! Over here!" others cried.

Henry began to streak towards the nearest star calling his name but stiffened when something began to pull him. Or push him. He couldn't tell which it was. He could tell only that the something was inside him. He looked at his chest, bewildered.

"Henry," Tess yelled. "Are you being...?"

"Pulled? Yeah."

"It's our hearts!" she yelled. "I think they know which stars to go to!"

"*Most* premium!" Henry exclaimed, more delighted than an elephant at a peanut farm.

Henry reached his first star before Tess did hers, and it began pulsating in time with his heartbeat. He brought his hands closer to it bit by bit until he gave it a gentle pat to test its temperature—it was bathwater warm. He curled his fingers around its edges and gave it a swift tug.

It didn't budge.

He readjusted his grip and pulled again. "Ugh!" he grunted. Still it didn't move.

"Dang it," Henry said. "Mine's not budging."

"Me either," Tess yelled back.

Put your feet on either side.
Push, pull, and pry.

Henry inspected the star more closely and noticed that the sky appeared darker, almost solid, around the edge of the star.

"OK. If you say so." Henry brought his feet up and placed them on either side of the star. The darker sky held his feet in place. "Sweet!"

He began pressing with his feet and pulling with his hands, huffing and puffing, until the star made a strange, tremendous sound—*Zzzzzank!*—and popped out of the sky. The force shot Henry back through space as if he were somersaulting down a hill. Except it was ten times more fun.

"Awesoooome!" Henry yelled as he floated back to where the star had been sitting.

The star had left in the sky a hole lined with a thin glittering film of stardust. Henry wiped his finger across it. The stardust bristled and sparked on his finger, and then jumped to the star he was holding.

At the same time, an inky blue-black liquid began seeping into the cavity the star had left, pushing the remaining stardust out one glistening speck at a time. Like a thousand shimmering grains of sand, the stardust began streaming to the star in Henry's hands. By the time the last grain had been reabsorbed, the hole had sealed over with a concrete blackness identical to the rest of the night.

"Got one," Henry yelled to Tess, who was now grunting and struggling with her feet propped on either side of her star.

Zzzzzank!

Tess tumbled back head over heels, heels over head, giggling and clutching her star.

"Me too!" She held up the star for him to see, her face glowing with exertion and thrill.

The two stars began singing a new song in unison.

"Hold me, hug me, right to your heart.
Then get ready for the very best part."

Henry looked at Tess. "You think it's OK?" he said.

"They were part of our hearts, right? It should be OK...I think...probably."

"All right then. Here goes," Henry said. He brought his star to his chest. It was toasty and comforting, like when his mom put a thick heavy blanket over him on a cold night. He gave the star a firm hug.

"Whoa! Tess, check this out!"

Tess floated by with her star in her hands. "No way. *Super* cool," she exclaimed.

The star was soaking right through his shirt, then right through his skin. Henry heard it whisper, "Home, home. Heart is where the home is."

"It kinda tickles," he said, and couldn't help giggling as the star finished soaking in. "But it feels so cool. It's better than when Mom tucks me in at night," he said with a big sigh. "Or chocolate ice cream. Or even hanging out in my tree house with Dad."

Tess immediately hugged her star and let it soak in.

"It's like...I don't know," she said with a big satisfied grin. "Fuzzy and warm all over, like a whole bunch of puppies are curled up inside me or something."

Henry nodded and they began racing from star to star. They zoomed and they whooped. They zipped and they looped. They crisscrossed the sky, flying hither and thither, stopping only long enough to pop out the closest stars calling their names and hug them back into their hearts.

After pulling, popping, hugging, and tumbling for a very long time, Tess slowed and said, "It looks like we're almost done."

"This is my last one," Henry said, dislodging a super-stuck star and tumbling gleefully through space.

Tess found her final star not much later on the far side of a yellow- and black-striped planet that according to the large banner plastered across its surface was named Yonzibar. Watching her hug it into her heart, Henry noticed she had a soft glow about her, as if she were now a star herself. He looked at his hands. They had a similar hazy glimmer.

Tess flitted over to Henry. Despite all the effort it'd taken to reclaim their stars, she looked rested and peaceful, as if she'd just woken up from a very agreeable nap.

"There's this place," she began, all smiles and sparkly-eyed. "It's my favorite place ever. It's this field, and it's all full of sunflowers. I love going there and lying down with all the flowers towering over me, watching the clouds float by." She put her hands on her chest. "This is like that but a million trillion times better."

Henry nodded and imagined his own favorite place. It was on top of a big flat rock that sat in a clearing deep in the woods, by a creek. He had the strange sensation of that place now floating inside him, in of his heart. "No more lying or being mean or calling people names for me."

"Me neither," said Tess with conviction. "Let's make a pact."

"What do you mean?"

"Like, if you forget and you're about to call me an ugly crawdad or something, I'll tell you. And if I forget and I'm about to cuss or call you snail legs or something like that, you tell me."

"Deal," Henry said. "We need a code word. So no one else will know what we're talking about."

"Totally!" said Tess.

"How about *Yonzibar?*" Henry said.

"Or *sunflowers!*" Tess countered.

"*Zorkalork conquerors!*" Henry exclaimed, pointing a finger in the air.

"*Baton!*" Tess said, raising her baton.

"*Eye patch!*"

They paused, looked at each other sideways, and smiled.

"*Ray!*" they said in unison, and Henry decided then and there that whatever cooties were, they couldn't be all that bad if someone like Tess had them. He spat in his hand. She spat in her hand. And they shook.

"But what about if someone is mean to us? Like Cassandra," Tess said. "I'm pretty sure she's going to keep being mean. Do you think there is a way to hold on to those stars?"

"I don't know," Henry said, giving it some thought. "But maybe it's like the canyon. Remember the canyon said it held in all the angry and painful stuff and wished it hadn't, and that made it crack? Maybe it's the same for the stars. They crack off of our hearts if we hold in all the hurting stuff!"

Tess jumped in, excited, and said, "I bet you're right. That makes total sense! Telling someone about it probably acts like a star bandaid or something and keeps it from cracking off. That is so cool!"

"I think I'd feel weird about doing that," said Henry.

"Nah," Tess replied. "You could tell me or your Mom or Dad. Y'know, someone you trust and stuff. They won't think it's weird. Or at least I know I wouldn't. And anyway, I'd rather feel weird then lose another star."

"Yeah, that's true. Me too," Henry said, deciding he would definitely try it. "Anyway, so how do you think we get home?"

Henry was not worried. He was not afraid. Instead his voice was calm, confident, and matter of fact.

Tess gave him a blank stare. "Jeesh, I have no idea."

They looked around. All they could see were planets and moons and stars. There was no sign of a spaceship or a black hole or any other possible way to leave.

Rotating like a planet, Henry looked around and racked his brain for a solution, idly putting his hands in his pockets. Deep in one, he felt what he thought was a marble or a locket. It took him a moment to realize it was Lion's bell.

He spun towards Tess and showed her.

"Nice *pink* bell," she joked.

"It's not mine," Henry said flatly. "It's Lion's. She said that if I really got stuck, I should ring it and holler."

"*Holler?*" said Tess. "Who says *holler?*"

"Lion, I guess," Henry said, shrugging his shoulders.

"Wait a second. Your cat told you this?" Tess said. Henry could tell she doubted him.

"Remember, I told you how I got here, and, hello, we just flew around space pulling stars out of the sky and hugging them into us, after a bubble-blowing talking bear who wore a bathrobe and an eye patch helped us get here," Henry said.

"Right, right. Good point. Why am I still doubting anything?" Tess laughed. "OK then, what are you supposed to *holler?*"

"I have completely, absolutely, positively zero idea. Lion just said whatever comes out." Henry cleared his throat and began ringing the bell. He opened his mouth and out popped "Hello, Lion, come in. Come

in, Lion."

Nothing happened.

Tess said, "I don't think it's a walkie-talkie."

Henry kept going: "Hello? Lion. Come in, Lion."

He continued to ring the bell until Tess said, "Maybe it's broken or something." However, she'd barely uttered the word *something* when a voice rose from the dark void of space. It said, "Copy that. I have you on the horn now."

A cluster of nearby stars began jibbing and jiving. They looked like a hive's worth of giant white bees swarming through space. As they settled back down, an enormous outline of Lion appeared, pinned to the sky.

"Lion!" Henry said, delighted.

"Hello and—*meow*—how do they say it, copy that, good buddy," Lion said. Her lips buzzed and crackled with light as she spoke.

Tess, who realized the bell did act like a walkie-talkie, giggled and said, "My bad."

"Are you two all right? You both have a truly ravishing glow about you," Lion said.

Tess replied, "We're great! We're like way better than OK. We've got all our stars and we want to go home, but we have zero clue how to do it."

"Oh," Lion said. "That's easy. Although I suppose it will be easy only once you know how to do it." She swished her tail across the night sky, it glittered and popped with light like a Fourth of July sparkler. "Henry, I see you still have your leaf. Excellent. I told you you'd need it."

"No kidding," Henry said, nodding and remembering how the leaf had saved him in the river. Then, remembering what had come next, he added, "But hey, you said there weren't any zorkalorks!" Henry felt the red edge of anger rising inside him. "You said the coast was clear! I almost got eaten!"

Lion remained calm. "No, I distinctly said the coast was clear *under* your bed. I made no claims whatsoever about what you might encounter beyond that."

The heated wind inside Henry popped and deflated. Lion was right. Henry made a noise that sounded like a motorboat running out of gas, and lobbed his head from side to side, conceding the point.

"Now then," Lion said, "both of you hold onto the leaf."

Henry slung the leaf off his back, and they each grabbed hold of one side.

"Next, although I do wish there were a more dignified way to do this, spit on it."

"Spit?" said Tess.

"Yes. Spit. Both of you. As big as you can. It needs some sort of water, after all."

They spat.

The leaf began to grow in their hands.

"Keep spitting," said Lion.

Henry and Tess began spitting as much as they could.

Spit. Spit. Spit. Spat. Spat. Spit. Spit. Spat. Spit.

It kept growing until it was five times its original size and the jump rope was pulling up its sides so it looked something like a basket. "There you go. That's it. That's all. Now take a seat up on top and be sure to enjoy the drop."

"The drop?" Tess said as they climbed into the leaf.

"Lion, you're rhyming again," Henry said.

But the stars were swarming like bees once more, and when they stopped, Lion was gone.

"What do you think she meant by 'the drop'?" Tess said as they prepared themselves.

"I have no idea," Henry said. "But it's probably gonna be crazy."

They clasped the side of the leaf and hunkered down. But, instead of dropping like a rock, the leaf began to gently drift and spiral down, just as a leaf does when it falls from a tree.

"Not so crazy," Tess said, shrugging.

"Not so much," Henry said, disappointed.

They relaxed back onto the leaf. Around them quasars were pulsating, planets were rotating, comets were shooting past, and millions of stars were floating up past them, securing themselves into the sky.

Tess said, "There are so many stars. Like a gazillion bazillion. They must all belong to someone, right?"

"Yeah," Henry said, straining his head back to watch a meteor drop behind them.

"So how long do you think the stars have to wait?"

Henry thought for a while. "Depends on the person, I guess."

"Yeah, probably," Tess said. "I bet Cassandra's stars are going to have to wait a really long time." There was a touch of sadness in her voice.

Henry knew how she was feeling, because even though he felt incredibly light and happy, a tiny stone of sadness had just formed deep in his ribs. This sadness wasn't like when someone called him "Cornball" or "klutzoid" or when he got grounded. This sadness was for all the people who didn't have their stars.

Tess touched the bruise on her arm and said, "I can't believe I'm going to say this, but I think I feel sorry for her."

Henry nodded in agreement and tried to imagine what the world would be like if everyone had their stars. The leaf, however, was drifting back and forth like a metronome, and it was more comfortable than his bed. Soon his tired eyelids were drooping shut, and it wasn't long until he and Tess fell asleep.

Chapter 15

Henry shook with a start. The strong thump of his heart had woken him, and sitting up, he discovered he was in his own bed. Morning light was pouring in through his window.

Stretching and gazing around the room, he saw his sheets and pillows were piled in a mountainous mound in the center of the bed. His jump rope and pencil lay on the floor. His flashlight was in the drawer, which was as messy as ever. His leaf was tacked on the wall exactly where it had always hung.

"Tess?" he whispered, even though he knew she wasn't there.

He jumped out of the bed and looked under it. There was not even a hint of water, only lint and a dry piece of clay.

He raised his eyebrows and shook his head, thinking how it had all seemed so real. He remembered the river and the zorkalorks and Ray and the canyon and the mountain and the stars and Tess. He let out a *humph* of disappointment.

Still, he knew what he had to do. He walked out of his room, past the ratty sock full of catnip, and through the hallway, where all the evidence of the shattered snow globe had been cleaned up. He found his parents in the

living room reading on the couch. Pieces from inside the snow globe lay on a table by the end of the couch. Seeing the busted-up rams and geese strengthened Henry's resolve.

He said, "Mom. Dad. I lied."

His mom looked up from the book she was reading. It was titled *How to Kill a Rock Star,* and its cover was fire-engine red. She said, "What do you mean, honey?"

Lion was curled in a ball at her feet. The cat glanced at Henry but then closed her eyes and appeared to fall asleep.

Henry straightened his shoulders and said, "I broke the snow globe. It wasn't Lion. I was chasing her and I was running in the house and I know I'm not supposed to run in the house and you've told me a million times not to run in the house, but I was and I ran into the table and I broke it. And I'm really, really, *really* sorry."

He was sure his mom and dad were going to get mad, but he wasn't done talking. He wanted to finish before they said anything. He added, "And I promise to get it fixed, even if it takes until I'm like one hundred and three. And I'll use my allowance and mow lawns and wash cars and stuff like that to pay for it."

He looked from his mom to his dad trying to gauge their reaction, but he was not nervous. He was not afraid.

"Henry, you just made us so happy," his mom said, smiling.

"Huh?" said Henry. "I did?"

"We knew it was you. We knew that you'd lied," his dad said.

"You did?"

"Of course," said his mom.

"You're not a very good liar," his dad added. "You never look us in the eyes when you're lying. Last night was disappointing, to say the least."

Henry's mom nodded in agreement. "But, last night we decided we'd wait to see if you'd admit it."

"And now," his dad continued, "here you are, telling the truth and promising to fix it. You're taking responsibility and being honest. I'm proud of you."

"So I'm not in trouble?" Henry said, shocked. It crossed his mind that this might not really be happening either.

His mom replied, "Well, you can certainly keep your promise to get it fixed. It'll need a new glass globe, and the mountain might need to be replaced. Luckily, you *should* be able to save enough money for that long before you're one hundred and three. Still, I don't want to tell you again..."

"No running in the house," Henry said in unison with his mom. "Check!" He'd always thought the whole no-running-in-the-house thing was stupid, but she'd been right all along.

"And one more thing," his mom said. "Have you seen Lion's bell anywhere?"

Henry immediately thought of one place it might be. He reached into his pocket and dug around. His heart jumped when he touched something that felt sort of like a locket. He pulled the object out and opened his hand.

Resting in his palm was a yellow- and black-striped marble. It looked like the planet Yonzibar.

"Darn it," he whispered, disappointed. Last night had all been a dream. He looked at his mom. "No, I don't know where it is."

His mom reached down, scratched Lion between the ears, and in a singsong voice said, "What'd you do with that bell, you cwazy cat?" Lion purred and kept her eyes closed, not opening them even when a *knock-knock-knock* came from the front door. Henry's mom looked back at him. "Will you get that, honey?"

Henry opened the door. Sparkling white sunlight flooded the room, and there, in its glow, stood Tess with a strange look on her face.

"Hey," she said.

"Hey," Henry echoed.

She held out her fist and opened her hand. Lion's bell lay in her palm. "I found this when I woke up. It was caught on my shirt."

Henry's eyes bulged and his head dropped towards the bell. They turned to look at Lion as the bell jingled across Tess's palm. The cat casually opened one eye, then the other.

"But that means...," Henry said, glancing at Tess, then back at Lion.

Lion lifted her head, winked at them, and said, "*Meow.*"

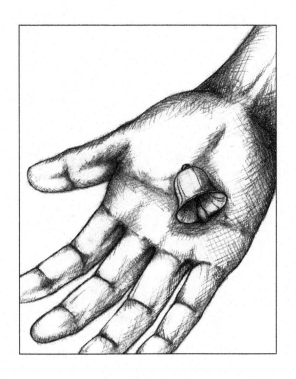

The End

CPSIA information can be obtained at www.ICGtesting.com
Printed in the USA
LVOW05s2230040815

448887LV00007B/46/P